TRICK

OR

Treat

Other Ellora's Cave Anthologies
Available from Pocket Books

GOOD GIRL SEEKS BAD RIDER
by Vonna Harper, Lena Matthews, & Ruth D. Kerce

ROAD TRIP TO PASSION
by Sahara Kelly, Lani Aames, & Vonna Harper

OVERTIME, UNDER HIM
by N. J. Walters, Susie Charles, & Jan Springer

GETTING WHAT SHE WANTS
by Diana Hunter, S. L. Carpenter, & Chris Tanglen

INSATIABLE
by Sherri L. King, Elizabeth Jewell, & S. L. Carpenter

HIS FANTASIES, HER DREAMS
by Sherri L. King, S. L. Carpenter, & Trista Ann Michaels

MASTER OF SECRET DESIRES
by S. L. Carpenter, Elizabeth Jewell, & Tawny Taylor

BEDTIME, PLAYTIME
by Jaid Black, Sherri L. King, & Ruth D. Kerce

HURTS SO GOOD
by Gail Faulkner, Lisa Renee Jones, & SAhara Kelly

LOVER FROM ANOTHER WORLD
by Rachel Carrington, Elizabeth Jewell, & Shiloh Walker

FEVER-HOT DREAMS
by Sherri L. King, Jaci Burton, & Samantha Winston

TAMING HIM
by Kimberly Dean, Summer Devon, & Michelle M. Pillow

ALL SHE WANTS
by Jaid Black, Dominique Adair, & Shiloh Walker

TRICK
OR
Treat

N. J. WALTERS
JAN SPRINGER
CHARLENE TEGLIA
TAWNY TAYLOR

POCKET BOOKS
New York   London   Toronto   Sydney

Pocket Books
A Division of Simon & Schuster, Inc.
1230 Avenue of the Americas
New York, NY 10020

First Pocket Books trade paperback edition October 2009

POCKET and colophon are registered trademarks of Simon & Schuster, Inc.

For information about special discounts for bulk purchases, please contact Simon & Schuster Special Sales at 1-800-456-6798 or business@simonandschuster.com

The Simon & Schuster Speakers Bureau can bring authors to your live event. For more information or to book an event contact the Simon & Schuster Speakers Bureau at 866-248-3049 or visit our website at www.simonspeakers.com.

Designed by Renata Di Biase

Manufactured in the United States of America

10 9 8 7 6 5 4 3 2 1

Library of Congress Cataloging-in-Publication Data

Trick or treat / N.J. Walters . . . [et al.].
   p. cm
  1. Erotic stories, American. I. Walters, N. J.
PS648.E7T75 2009
813'60803538—dc22   2009002736

ISBN 978-1-4391-3155-8

These stories have previously appeared in Ellora's Cave anthologies published by Pocket Books. "Unmasking Kelly" appeared in *Overtime, Under Him.* "Sinderella" appeared in *Bad Girls Have More Fun.* "Wolf in Cheap Clothing" appeared in *Out of This World Lover.* "Stolen Goddess" appeared in *Naughty Nights.*

Contents

TRICK
OR
Treat

Unmasking Kelly

N. J. WALTERS

DEDICATION

*To my friends on the Playground, especially Kelly,
thank you so much for your unwavering support,
your good humor and friendship. You ladies are
the best!*

*Also, thank you to my new editor, Mary Altman,
for your hard work and guidance on this first
project we have ever worked on together. Mary, you
made edits fun. Now that's a talent!*

*To my wonderful husband who is always supportive
and loving no matter what I do. I couldn't do it
without you.*

Chapter 1

Kelly Allen stared at her reflection in the bar window. She almost glanced over her shoulder to see if there was someone standing behind her, for the woman staring back was unrecognizable.

The wind whipped up, sending a gust billowing under her voluminous skirt. Batting it down with one hand, she gripped the lapels of her coat tighter around her upper body. She'd borrowed the coat from her friend and it was too small and didn't quite close properly. A shiver raced down her spine. It wasn't so much the cold, although it was a cool, damp night. It was more a combination of fear and anticipation that held her captive as she continued to examine the woman reflected in the window.

It was a shadowy image at best. The streetlights and the muted glow from the surrounding businesses were the only illumination. It had rained earlier in the evening but now it was just a light drizzle. Puddles filled the streets and Kelly curled her toes in her impractical high-heeled shoes.

Although the reflection was dim, she knew all too well what she looked like. She was still amazed at the transformation her friend Lori had wrought in one afternoon. Kelly had curly, shoulder-length auburn hair that she usually kept ruthlessly pulled back in a severe bun, but Lori had styled the thick mass and added some kind of gel to it. Now it was artfully tousled, falling around her shoulders.

That wasn't all her friend had done. Kelly never wore much makeup beyond a swipe of mascara and a slick of nearly nude lipstick, but Lori had added eye shadow and eyeliner and now Kelly's blue eyes looked deep and mysterious. A touch of color on her cheeks actually made her look like she had cheekbones and a rich plum lipstick accentuated her full lips. It was amazing how some makeup and a new hairdo changed her look.

But Lori hadn't been finished by any means. Her friend had poked and prodded her until she'd donned the outfit that they'd decided on. Kelly hadn't been so sure, but her friend had been insistent, so Kelly had reluctantly squeezed her size sixteen body into a tight bustier and a many-layered skirt that fell to just below her knees.

The bustier was mostly black with red trim and laces running up the front. It cupped her breasts, pushing the already large 36 D-cup mounds even higher. Kelly had to fight the urge to keep tugging at the front of her top. She'd never worn anything cut so low in her life. If she bent over too far, she was afraid her nipples would show. But she had to admit that her cleavage was impressive.

The skirt was made of a silky material that matched the bustier. Layers of crinoline beneath it caused a swishing sound when she walked. A hint of red peeked out from beneath the hem of the skirt. Black fishnet thigh-high stockings and high-heeled shoes completed her ensemble.

Kelly was a tall, sturdy girl standing a shade below six feet in her stocking feet. With the three-inch heels that Lori had insisted she wear, Kelly felt like a giant. But even she would admit that she looked different. With her waist cinched in and her breasts accentuated, she looked, well, almost sexy. It was so unlike her that she'd kept checking the mirror at home until Lori had finally pushed her out the door and into the waiting cab.

Her fingers clenched as she pulled away from her reflection. Material crinkled as she looked down at the most important piece of her costume—her mask. It too was black and trimmed with red and covered most of her forehead and nose. Combined with her makeover, it would easily conceal enough of her face to mask her true identity. Without it, she'd never have the nerve to attempt what she was about to do. Placing a hand on her stomach to try to calm her jittery nerves, she took a deep breath and slowly released it. She, Kelly Allen, was about to walk into Brannigan's Pub and seduce the owner, Liam Brannigan.

Liam Brannigan was the stuff of women's fantasies. He had hair so black it looked almost blue in some lights and he wore it long and loose around his shoulders. His eyes were the same dark blue as a night sky and a perpetual shadow covered his chin, giving him a sexy, just-got-out-of-bed look that had caught more than one woman's eye.

And that was even before you got to his body. His shoulders had to be almost a yard wide and his massive chest tapered down to a lean waist. His legs were long and muscular and the way he filled out a pair of jeans ought to be illegal. At six-foot-four, he was even taller than she was. And in Kelly's experience, that didn't happen very often.

Just the mere thought of him had her breasts swelling and her nipples puckering. She could feel them pressing against the stiff fabric of the bustier and it took all her willpower not to press her hands against them to help ease the ache. Her panties were already damp with need. She could feel the cream slipping from her body as she pictured Liam in a pair of tight jeans and nothing else. Kelly gulped back air to try to calm herself.

She'd been working as a waitress at Brannigan's for more than a year now. Most people didn't seem to think of it as a profession but Kelly had long ago decided that, not only did she like it, she was proficient enough at it to make decent money. At twenty-six, she was settled and content with her life. She enjoyed her job, her friends and her hobbies. She didn't date much and hadn't had a serious relationship in two years. Most men were put off by her height, her weight or both. Kelly tried to convince herself that she didn't care but it still stung.

Brannigan's was a neighborhood pub. They opened at eleven, just in time for the lunch crowd, and closed at one o'clock in the morning. They served both lunch and supper— mostly sandwich platters and soups. The rest of the day, they served pub snacks. And, of course, the beer flowed freely all day long. It wasn't a rowdy place but, rather, a comfortable one. They had a lot of regular customers and were a favorite hangout in the neighborhood.

Personally, Kelly thought that many of the female patrons flocked there just for the chance to glimpse Liam. And who could blame them? Liam's good nature and his easy, friendly manner attracted both males and females alike, while his sheer size kept the occasional drunk or problem customer in line.

A door opened and closed and the noise from the bar filtered out onto the street. The annual Halloween Masquerade party was under way and had been for quite some time. It was already close to midnight. Liam hadn't been too happy with her when she'd asked for the day off, but since she'd worked all the holiday shifts since she came to Brannigan's Pub, he had agreed. She really hadn't liked leaving him short-handed for the party but Lori had insisted that she'd need the time to work her magic on Kelly.

In the end, Kelly had gone in at nine this morning and left at three in the afternoon. That way, she'd been able to take care of most of the preparations for the party as well as cover the lunch crowd. People had been in a celebratory mood during lunch and many of the patrons had been planning on coming back for the party. Several of them had asked if she was going to be at the party, but she'd told them that she had other plans for the evening. Liam had continued to scowl at her every time she'd said that. It had only added to her guilt.

But she'd done it anyway. It was her own fault she was in this predicament. One night not so long ago, she'd had one too many glasses of wine and spilled her well-kept secret to

Lori. For more than a year, she'd secretly yearned to seduce her boss. It was more than just that, though. After working side-by-side with Liam for a year, Kelly knew that he was everything she'd ever wanted in a man. Hardworking and loyal, he inspired the same in his staff. His humor was infectious and he had a basic honesty about him that was very appealing. They shared many of the same views on things but had enough differences to keep it interesting.

But Liam was not a settling-down kind of man. At thirty-two, he owned his own business, had good friends and plenty of interests. He never lacked for female companionship but he never had a serious relationship. He worked hard and he played hard. The fact that he lived in an apartment above the bar meant that he worked long hours and he always teased that no woman would put up with that. But Kelly knew better. If there was no woman in his life, it was by his own choice.

That was fine with her. She was under no illusion that she could attract and keep a man like Liam, but she could take this shot at a one-night stand. Hot, grinding, sweaty sex was just what she needed according to Lori. And after many restless nights dreaming about Liam, Kelly was finally willing to agree with her. She might not get forever, but she would have this one night with him. That was, if she could work up enough nerve to open the door and go inside.

It had all seemed so simple back at her apartment with Lori goading her on—she'd dress up in a sexy outfit, put on her mask, saunter into the bar and seduce Liam. It was only now she realized just how many flaws there were in her flimsy plan.

Number one, she couldn't saunter in her high-heeled shoes. Used to wearing flats or sneakers, Kelly had been practicing walking in her shoes for days. But as hard as she tried, she still tottered on her heels. The first pair of shoes Lori had pressed on her had been a disaster. Kelly had been unable to even stand up in the four-inch, impossibly skinny heels. Lori had relented and they'd settled on a pair of black three-inch heels with open toes and a slender strap that wrapped around her foot. It had taken a lot of practice but at least she could walk in them, and even she admitted that they made her feel sexy.

Problem number two was she didn't really know how to go about seducing a man. Yes, she'd dated, but she'd never purposely set out to seduce anyone into having a one-night fling. In fact, she'd never had one in her life. The two men she'd had sexual relationships with had been men she'd dated seriously for several months before she'd actually slept with them.

And problem three was that underneath the sexy saloon girl costume, she was still Kelly Allen—tall, overweight and not very confident in the sexual arena. She chewed uncertainly on her lip and immediately stopped when she realized she was wearing away her lipstick. A part of her longed to run home, haul off the costume, and wrap herself in her flannel pajamas, but another part of her wanted to reach out and take a chance at getting what she wanted. And she definitely wanted Liam Brannigan. Besides, her cab was long gone and it would be almost impossible to hail another on a busy night like tonight.

A man in a cowboy hat, denim shirt and tight jeans

sauntered by. He stopped, turned and stared at her, emitting an almost soundless whistle as he did so. Kelly was shocked when he slowly ran his eyes up and down her body. His lips turned up in a slow, welcoming smile. "Well howdy, sweetheart." He tipped back his hat with his index finger as his smile grew wider. "Are you going to the party?"

It was now or never. Slipping her mask down over her eyes, she adjusted it so that it was comfortable. In the soft, sultry voice that she'd been practicing, she smiled at the cowboy. "I believe I will."

He reached out and pulled open the door to Brannigan's, motioning her forward with a sweep of his arm. "After you, beautiful lady."

Placing one foot in front of the other, Kelly took the steps that led her from the cool, damp street and into the waiting party.

Chapter 2

The combination of intense heat, laughter and Celtic music assaulted her senses as she entered the room. Although the lights weren't bright, they seemed harsh after the darkness outside. She blinked several times before her eyes adjusted. A large hand pressed against the base of her spine, making her jump.

"Whoa there, sugar," the cowboy whispered in her ear. "Just don't want the crowd to run you over." It was a logical explanation, as the pub was packed to capacity, but Kelly could feel the heat even through the layers of her coat and costume.

Taking a tiny step away from him, she looked around the bar, a feeling of pleasure and satisfaction filling her as she watched the throng of people enjoying themselves. She and some of the other staff had worked all morning decking out the bar and it had definitely been worth all the time they'd put into it. Orange and purple lights were strung around the bar and carved pumpkins sat in the center of each table with lights shining through their slanted eyes and crooked mouths. Rather than hire a band, they'd had a DJ set up in one corner so that the music would be continuous all night long. The top of the pool table had been covered with a large, festive tablecloth that was loaded down with pub snacks.

"Can I buy you a drink?" Kelly was surprised that the cowboy was still standing behind her. She really looked at him for the first time and was shocked to find that he was actually good-looking. With his cowboy boots, he was as tall as she was even with her heels.

But as great as he looked, he wasn't the man she wanted. "Thank you," she began regretfully but he held up a hand to stop her.

"No need, sugar. I knew a fine woman like you had to be taken." Reaching out, he lifted her hand and brought it to his mouth. "But if he disappoints you, you just come and find me." He placed a soft kiss on her knuckles before releasing her hand, turning and blending into the crowd.

Kelly knew that her mouth must be hanging open but she couldn't help it. Men didn't flirt with her. They just didn't. But she'd seen the honest appreciation in his eyes as he'd stared at her. His actions bolstered her spirits, giving her a renewed confidence. Slipping off her jacket, she headed toward the bar. She was grateful for the long, red silk gloves that covered her arms to just above her elbows. The bustier left her shoulders exposed and the gloves helped her feel not quite so naked.

The room was crowded with people and it took her a

while to work her way toward the bar at the far end where Liam was doling out drinks and conversation. An Elvis and a vampire waylaid her and it took her some time to convince them that she wasn't interested in their rather graphic proposals. Amused, perhaps, but not interested. Really, she'd gotten more indecent propositions tonight than she'd had in her entire life. She knew her outfit was sexy but this was just too much.

She heard him before she saw him. His laughter rang out across the bar, cutting through the music. The crowd seemed to part in front of her and she caught sight of him. She froze in place as he tipped back his head and laughed again at some jest a customer had made.

His long, black hair flowed down over his shoulders and she caught the glint of a diamond stud in his ear. The open neck of his crisp, white shirt framed the strong column of his neck. The shirt sleeves were long and billowy, ending in tight cuffs around his thick wrists. He looked every inch the pirate.

Moving like a sleepwalker in a dream, Kelly didn't quite know how she made it to the bar without tripping. She draped her coat over the back of an empty stool tucked away in a dimly lit corner on the far side of the bar. Sliding onto the seat, she propped her elbows on the edge of the bar, rested her chin in her hands and continued to stare at him.

His tight black jeans left nothing to the imagination, showcasing his muscular thighs and the impressive bulge of his cock. Black leather boots rose to his knees and he wore a dagger strapped to his side that looked incredibly real. The costume suited him perfectly.

She sighed as she ogled his tight butt, her fingers itching

to touch it, and she had to swallow her groan of disappointment when he turned around again. Although the front view was even better than the back. Truthfully, the man didn't have a bad side.

Liam worked his way down the bar, serving up tall, cold mugs of beer and mixing drinks until he finally reached her far corner. "Welcome to Brannigan's, pretty lady. What can I get you?" His smooth, deep tones rolled across her skin like a caress. He stood in front of her with his hands on his hips and a twinkle in those deep blue eyes. His shirt was open at the top, emphasizing the strong column of his neck and offering her a tantalizing glimpse of his impressive chest. Really, the man was too sexy to be let out amongst the regular population.

She frowned when she realized he was staring at her. Glancing down, she had a quick peek at her cleavage to make sure she hadn't fallen out of the bustier. It was close. Her breasts swelled against the lace trim, but her nipples were still covered. Barely.

Her head jerked up when she felt his fingers beneath her chin. But instead of releasing her, his hand cupped her jaw and he leaned closer. For a moment she thought he might kiss her. Her lips parted in anticipation. His breath was warm on her moist mouth. He was close. So very close.

"What can I get you?" His voice was so soft and seductive it took a few seconds for her to process the meaning of his words. She jerked her head back in embarrassment, her cheeks heating. While she'd been all but undressing the man with her eyes, he'd been waiting for her to order.

"White wine, please." Her tone was briskly matter-of-fact

and Kelly wanted to bang her head against the bar in frustration. She wasn't supposed to use her regular voice. She'd practiced lowering her voice and speaking more slowly and sensually.

But Liam had turned away to fill her drink order, giving no indication that he recognized her. Good. All wasn't lost. She could do this. She knew she could. When he placed her glass on the bar in front of her, she smiled at him. "Thank you, handsome." This time, her voice was mellow with a come-hither tone.

He smiled his pirate's grin. "You're welcome. You here with anyone?"

This was it. This was her chance. Trying not to seem too eager, she picked up her glass and took a long sip. Lowering the glass back to the bar, she licked her lips, allowing her tongue to stroke across first the upper and then the lower lip. His eyes tracked every movement of her tongue.

Was it just her or was the room getting hotter? Her costume suddenly seemed incredibly tight and she struggled to breathe. Her breasts felt so heavy and the tips ached unbearably. The tight lacing that cinched her waist and torso made her feel voluptuous and unbelievably sexy. Her pussy throbbed and she struggled not to squirm in her seat.

"No," she managed to whisper. "I'm not with anyone."

Liam leaned across the bar and stared into her eyes. The world around them disappeared. The sounds of the music, the chatter of the people and the din of the bar seemed to fade into nothing. There was only her and Liam. His lips barely skimmed hers before leaving a trail of hot, moist kisses to her ear. He traced the whorl of her ear with his tongue before nipping the lobe with his teeth. "You are now," he whispered. "If that's what you want."

Kelly gripped the bar with her hands to keep from slipping off her stool and melting onto the floor. Molten lava flowed through her veins. Need pulsed through her body unlike anything she'd ever experienced. Oh, yeah, she definitely wanted. She tried to speak but words were beyond her. She managed to nod her head in agreement but that was enough for Liam.

"Don't go anywhere, sweetheart." He gave her neck one final nuzzle before pulling away. "I've got to work but I'll be back."

Again, Kelly just nodded as he went back to serving up drinks. The pub's part-time bartender, Frank, joined him behind the counter and began to fill the waitresses' orders. Trying to regain her equilibrium, she turned sideways in her seat so she could watch the crowd. The waitresses moved easily through the throngs of people, carrying their trays loaded with drinks. She ruthlessly squashed her momentary feeling of guilt for not working tonight.

Resting one arm on the counter, she sipped her wine as she enjoyed the scene before her. The bar was alive with music and she tapped her toe as several lively tunes had the dance floor hopping. As the faster songs gave way to a slower one, the mood changed. Bodies moved closer, swaying in time. The lights flickered across many of the faces, giving them an exotic, otherworldly look. Hands groped and stroked as things got steamy between some of the partners.

Just watching them was making her hot. She could almost feel the stroke of a hand across her own back. Then she felt it again—a hard hand slid down the long line of her back, ending just above her behind. Startled, she whirled around, glaring at the offender. She'd been so caught up with the dancers she hadn't noticed anyone coming up beside her. It was her cowboy again and he was staring at her, totally unabashed and unrepentant.

"Hey, sugar. I thought you said you were here with someone." He laid his empty beer bottle on the counter next to her wineglass.

Kelly automatically glanced toward Liam and was surprised to find him only a few steps away with a scowl on his face. She hadn't realized that he was so close to her end of the bar. She opened her mouth to reply but before she could get the words out, Liam's deep, harsh voice cut her off. "The lady is with me." Kelly could only stare in wonder at Liam as he glared at the cowboy.

The cowboy stood tall and stared back at Liam, seemingly totally unafraid of his size or the potential threat he presented. Kelly could barely stand the tension that flowed between the two men. Finally, after what seemed an intolerable length of time but was probably no more than a few seconds, the cowboy tipped his head toward Liam.

Turning back to her, he smiled. Reaching into his back pocket, he drew out a business card and, without a word, tucked it safely into her coat pocket. As he stood, his lips grazed her ear. "Just in case it doesn't work out with him, sugar." He turned and sauntered toward the entrance, melting into the crowd. Kelly watched him until he disappeared from sight, catching a final glimpse of him as he opened the front door and left.

"Would you rather have gone with him?" Her attention snapped back to Liam, who was standing there looking like a thundercloud.

Kelly shook her head and licked her dry lips. "No. I'd rather be here with you."

"Are you sure, sweetheart?"

"Yes." Propping her elbows on the bar, she squeezed her arms against her sides, knowing that the simple action pushed her breasts even higher.

Liam's eyes glowed as he stared at the creamy mounds of her breasts. Her nipples tingled under his stare. "Prove it."

"What?" Now she was totally lost.

Liam leaned closer and ran a finger over the slope of a breast and dipped into her cleavage. Kelly didn't dare breathe until he'd withdrawn his hand. Her skin burned where he'd touched her. "Go to the ladies' room, take off your panties and bring them back to me."

"Are you nuts?" She was shocked and aroused by his suggestion. The conflicting emotions rocketed through her entire body. Her pussy was flooded with cream as she imagined herself seated on the barstool with no panties on.

"No. I want your pussy hot and wet for me by the time we close. I want you to want my cock in your body." His gaze scorched her with its heat. "I know your panties will be damp. They'll smell like you too—hot, musky and oh so inviting. You've already creamed your panties, haven't you, sweetheart?"

Kelly thought she'd come on the spot. No man had ever spoken to her in such a blatantly sexual manner before and she loved it. Determined not to let him totally have the upper hand, she parted her lips and flicked her tongue over her lip. "Yes, my panties are soaked." Her words were barely a whisper, but he definitely heard her. His eyes got even darker and he looked determined.

"I want them." His voice was thick with arousal. "You know you want to give them to me, don't you, sweetheart? Imagine how good you'll feel and how wet your pussy will get," he whispered as he leaned forward to trace the curve of her ear with his tongue. "If nothing else, it'll drive me crazy knowing you're naked underneath that incredible dress." He took a step back and she immediately missed his nearness. The corner of his mouth turned up in a grin but his eyes didn't reflect any humor. His entire body was tense as he waited for her decision.

Kelly had come too far to turn back now. She'd never seen Liam like this before, so blatantly sexual and demanding. While she had some experience in lovemaking, she'd never played sexual games with a partner before and found the possibility of indulging in them with Liam incredibly exciting and arousing. She wasn't about to stop now, not when she was finally so close to getting what she wanted.

Giving him what she hoped was a sultry smile, she slid off her barstool. "I'll be right back." Putting a sway in her hips, she walked toward the bathrooms. She could feel his eyes burning into her back with every step she took. When the door of the ladies' room closed behind her, she slumped back against the door. What in the heck had she just done?

Chapter 3

Liam watched his mystery lady leave, unable to tear his gaze away from the hypnotic sway of her hips. He could imagine gripping those hips from behind while he pounded his cock into her sweet pussy. He could almost hear the slap of his stomach against her ass as he took her. This was a real woman, full-figured and made to cradle a man of his size.

He'd noticed her the second she'd stepped through the doorway. She was tall and stood head and shoulders over most of the women and was even taller than many of the men. The light glinted off the reddish tones in her hair, making it shine like a jewel. And when she'd slipped off her coat, he'd almost swallowed his tongue. Her costume hugged her like a lover.

Her waist was cinched inward, accentuating the flare of her wide hips and the sheer magnificence of her breasts. The top of her outfit pushed her breasts high, leaving most of them exposed to view. Her creamy shoulders were bare but her hands and arms were covered by silky gloves. He'd never seen anything so sexy in his life. Just fantasizing about how that silk-covered hand would feel stroking his cock had caused it to swell to almost painful proportions. Liam had stuck close to the bar, trying his best to hide his erection from the customers seated there. He was thankful that most of them were wrapped up in their own business and were not paying him much attention.

No doubt about it. The lady was his and he hadn't hesitated to lay claim to her when she'd sat down. It had taken almost more restraint than he possessed to keep from hauling her up onto the bar, flipping up her skirt, pulling down her top and fucking her in front of everyone. He wanted to yell that she was his. He wanted to claim her in every way possible. And he damn well wasn't going to let some sweet-talking cowboy steal her away.

It was a good thing that he could practically tend bar in his sleep. He served customers and filled drink orders by rote, all the while keeping one eye on the door to the ladies' room. She'd been in there a long time. What if he'd pushed her too hard? What if she changed her mind? He'd almost lost it when the cowboy had left her his card and he had wanted her to prove that she belonged to him. Chauvinistic and primitive, he'd demanded her panties in compensation. Now he was afraid that she might run from him instead.

He heaved a huge breath of relief when the door finally opened and she stepped out. His mouth went dry as he imagined her flipping up the tail of her full skirt, hooking her fingers in her panties and dragging them down over her hips and legs. He could picture her bending down and slipping them over those sexy high-heeled shoes she was wearing. Had she really done it?

Yes, she had. He could tell by the nervous way she glanced around the room before heading toward the bar. Her legs were shaky as she wobbled on her shoes. He could see that her left hand was buried in the folds of her skirt.

Taking a deep breath, Liam forced himself to look away. If he wasn't careful, he'd come in his damned pants. His balls were so tight, he knew he was close. He was very aware of her smoothing her skirt under herself as she slipped back onto her stool but he continued to fill drink orders until he had some amount of control over his body again.

When he felt ready, he filled another glass with wine and placed it in front of her. "Compliments of the house, sweetheart." She nervously glanced around and chewed on her bottom lip. Liam wanted to howl with need. He wanted to lick that sweet lip before he claimed her mouth and sucked on that luscious tongue. "Do you have something for me?"

Her hand shot across the bar and he barely caught the small scrap of fabric before it slipped over the edge. Red satin filled his hand and he wrapped his fingers around it possessively. Angling his back so that no one could see what he was doing, he brought the fabric to his nose and drew in a deep breath. Her eyes dilated until they were almost black. He could see the arousal in her face and body as her breasts rose and fell quickly. Oh, yeah, his lady was as hot and bothered as he was.

"For now, it's your panties. I plan to touch and smell

and lick your hot pussy as soon as this bar is closed." Lifting the wineglass in his hand, he brought it to her mouth. She parted her lips and swallowed as he tipped the glass up. "Your mouth is so damn sexy. I can't wait to feel your lips wrapped around my cock, sucking it hard." When he'd lowered the glass back to the counter, he gave her one last, long stare. "Keep your legs spread wide apart, sweetheart. I want you primed and ready. I plan on fucking you long and hard."

He glanced at the clock as he went back to work. Only a half-hour left until closing. His shout of "last call" had folks hurrying up to the bar. Although he was busy, he was very aware of the woman waiting for him.

Kelly almost bolted and ran before the bar closed, but she'd come too far and she wanted this so very badly. Even though she was decently covered, she felt totally exposed.

Her legs were hooked around the sides of the barstool so that her sex was wide open but the folds of her skirt covered everything. Her breasts ached and when she looked down she could just see the edge of two rosy nipples peeking up at her. She resisted the urge to tug at her bustier. In the dimly lit corner where she sat, no one could see them but her, or Liam if he happened to come over.

But he'd been busy since she'd shoved her panties at him. She still couldn't believe that he'd sniffed them before stuffing them into his back pocket. And the things he'd said to her had sent waves of desire pulsing through her body. She was more than ready to be fucked long and hard, as he'd put it, but she was determined to fulfill some of her own fantasies first. This was her one and only opportunity to be with Liam and she planned to make the most of it.

When the door finally closed on the last customer and the last of the staff had departed, Liam shot the bolts home and turned off the main lights. Only the candles sputtering in the pumpkins and the strings of orange and purple lights illuminated the room. Kelly had pushed off her barstool while he'd been ushering out the last person. She took the change that she'd fished out of her coat pocket and fed it into the jukebox in the far corner of the bar. Pressing several buttons, she waited until a low, sexy beat began to pound from the speakers.

The staff had cleared the remains of the food from the pool table so Kelly flipped back the tablecloth that covered it. Rolling the cloth into a bundle, she dropped it onto the floor.

Liam walked toward her with a predatory gleam in his eye. With his long, black hair and superbly muscled physique, he resembled a large jungle cat on the prowl and she was definitely his prey. Kelly was more than willing to be caught, but not just yet.

She positioned two chairs as he moved toward her. When he showed no sign of stopping, she held up both hands. "Wait." He froze in place, but she could feel the sexual energy vibrating from him. She took a deep breath and took the plunge. "I want to dance for you first."

Liam stopped dead in his tracks when she held up her hands and told him to wait. His hands clenched into fists at his sides and every muscle in his body was poised for action. Had she changed her mind? He didn't think so. Her body language and lustful stare told him otherwise. But still he waited.

Her words stopped his heart for a brief moment before it began to slam hard against his chest. *She wanted to dance for him.* That was something he really wanted to see. The pounding of the music matched his heartbeat as she made her way to the chair she'd positioned next to the pool table.

She raised one foot and placed it on the chair. Her skirt slid upward, revealing a long, lush leg covered in fishnet. He'd soon find out if she was wearing a garter belt or thigh-high stockings. His entire body tightened in anticipation. She bit her lip uncertainly and it occurred to him just how awkward it would be for her to climb in heels.

Hastening to her side, he offered her his hand. The smile she gave him was filled with sensual promise as she stepped up onto the chair and, from there, moved to the top of the pool table. Liam really didn't want to let go of her but did so when she gave her hand a slight tug.

"Why don't you have a seat, relax and enjoy the show?" She waved her hand toward the other chair she'd positioned about four feet from the table.

Liam strode to the chair and dropped down into it. Flicking open the cuffs of his shirt, he rolled up the sleeves. When he finished, he crossed his arms over his chest, spread his long legs out in front of him and hooked one booted ankle over the other. Cocking an eyebrow at her, he waited.

He could tell she was nervous but determined. At first her movements were a little jerky and shaky, but the longer she swayed to the music, the more fluid they became. Raising her shapely arms in the air, she swung her hips from side to side. Slowly, she lowered her hands, running them down her neck and exposed chest. The red silk gloves were in stark contrast with her pale skin.

Lovingly, she cupped her breasts in her hands. He could just see the tips of her nipples peeking out of the bustier. He licked his lips, longing to taste them, to suckle them, to pleasure them. Reaching down, he adjusted his erection but there was no comfort to be found.

Her clever fingers dipped into her bodice and flicked at the puckered tips of her breasts. She shivered with desire at her own touch. It was amazingly arousing to watch her pleasure herself but he wanted more. "Keep going, sweetheart," he encouraged.

She moved her hips enticingly with each beat of the music. Sliding her hands down over her torso, she gripped the sides of her skirt and, with each movement, pulled the fabric higher. Liam sat up straight and leaned forward as the tops of her stockings came into view. "I knew you'd be wearing thigh-highs," he murmured as she continued to tease him with glimpses of her plump, white thighs.

Reaching into his back pocket, he pulled out her panties and rubbed the silk against his cheek. She moaned and undulated her hips. "Show me your pussy, sweetheart."

Her skirt dropped back down around her body as her hands disappeared behind her back. Then she raised her hands back to her breasts, cupping and kneading them as she pushed the bustier lower, releasing them from the confining fabric. With her skirt unzipped, every sway of her body shifted it lower. First her bellybutton was exposed, then her hipbones. Fuck, he'd never seen anything this erotic. With one final shimmy, the fabric fell to the table beneath her. Stepping away from the froth of material, she kicked it to one side.

The dark wood of the pool table gleamed in the dim lights. Like some sensual dream, she continued to move sinuously on the green felt top. Her hair was tousled and sexy, her eyes and part of her face covered by her black-and-red silk mask. The full lips that he longed to devour were parted. The bustier was still wrapped around her waist and torso but her breasts were totally exposed. Big and full and crowned with large, rosy tips that were puckered into tight buds, they were magnificent.

Her hips flared wide and her stomach had a gentle slope that invited his hand to trace the contours. Her long legs were covered in sexy, black fishnet stockings that exposed only her upper thighs. Her feet were arched in those tall heels that he found so sexy. What did women call them? Fuck-me shoes? Well, they were certainly working. He couldn't wait to fuck her.

But it was her pussy that drew his attention. The nest of hair at the apex of her thighs was the same lush color as her hair. Curly and soft, he wanted to run his fingers through it before parting her slick folds and sinking his fingers into her hot depths. As she moved to the music, he glimpsed the wetness on her thighs and pubic hair. She was hot and ready for him.

He didn't think it could get any more erotic than this. Then she bent over and picked up a cue stick.

Chapter 4

Kelly could barely keep her balance on the table. The way Liam was staring at her was making her legs weak. When he stared at her pussy and licked his lips, she almost dropped to the table, spread her legs and begged him to taste her. She'd probably do that too, but not yet.

Her inner core was pulsing in time to the music as one song ended and another began. She felt totally unlike her normal self. She felt sexy, self-assured and very erotic. Like some exotic creature, she could do things the normal Kelly wouldn't even dream of. With that in mind, she bent over and picked up a cue stick that had been pushed against the side of the table.

Straightening, she stepped to the edge closest to Liam. Planting the stick firmly on the table, she fitted the front of her body against it. Then, using the stick for support and leverage, she spread her feet wide, bent her knees and slowly slid the lower half of her body down the cue. It wasn't exactly a stripper's pole, but it was close enough.

Liam's eyes were glued to her pussy as she pulled herself back up. The smooth wood of the stick pressed against her swollen clit with every movement of her body. Cream flowed from her inner core as she repeated the motion several more times. Closing her eyes, she pushed her pussy harder against the wooden cue stick as she bent her knees again and began the slow journey down.

"Fuck." Her eyes popped open when Liam cursed. Still staring at her, he dragged his shirt over his head and dropped it to the floor. She could see the sheen of sweat on his chest, matting the light sprinkling of hair that spread from nipple to nipple before angling downward in a thin line and disappearing into the waistband of his pants.

But he wasn't finished. He practically tore the button off his jeans in his haste to open them. She discovered to her delight that he wasn't wearing any underwear when his cock sprang free from its confinement. Long and thick, the plum-shaped head was red from arousal. As she watched, fluid seeped from the slit. Wrapping his hand around the base, he held his erection and gave it one hard pump before releasing it.

Kelly decided it was time to make another one of her fantasies come true.

Falling to her knees, she discarded the cue stick. Pulling herself to the edge of the table, she swung her legs over the side. She pushed herself off the table and took the two steps necessary to bring her right in front of him. Then she began to move again.

Carefully, she twirled and stepped to his side. Leaning down, she rubbed one of her breasts against his arm as she blew in his ear. He reached out his hand but before he could touch her, she'd scooted behind him. Sinking her fingers into his scalp, she massaged the top of his head. Liam practically purred as she continued to run her fingers though the silky strands of his hair.

Shifting again, she flitted around to his other side, nipping at his neck and ears before moving on. Dancing her way back in front of him, she threw one leg over his lap and lowered herself onto his hard thighs. Then she did what she'd wanted to do for an entire year. Leaning forward, Kelly kissed him. Skimming her lips across his, she had her first taste of Liam—hot and masculine, with just the slightest taste of whiskey. Using her tongue, she traced first his top and then his bottom lip.

Liam's hand cupped her head, holding her steady as he plunged his tongue into her mouth. Taking his time, he explored and withdrew then forged into her mouth again. There was no part of her mouth that he didn't stroke or taste. Kelly had been kissed many times in her life, but never like this. This was a claiming on the most basic level.

Holding her still for his kiss with one hand, he brushed the tip of her breast with the other. Kelly shivered. "Tell me your name, mystery lady?" he whispered roughly.

For a moment, panic threatened to overwhelm her. No. There was no way he could find out who she was. There was no future for them and she didn't want to risk either their friendship or her job. Tears welled in her eyes and she started to pull away.

As if he sensed her turmoil, he began to soothe her immediately. "Shh, sweetheart. You don't have to tell me." He peppered her face with kisses as he cupped both her breasts with his hands and gently flicked the swollen nubs with his thumbs. His cock was rock-hard against her stomach as she pushed herself closer to him. "It's enough that you're here with me now."

His lips covered hers and all her worries were buried once more, replaced by the desire that always pulsed so close to the surface whenever she was around him. She had to give herself a mental shake to remind herself what she'd set out to do.

When he skimmed his fingers down her stomach toward her throbbing sex, she knew that if she didn't move now, she'd lose her only chance to do this. Putting both hands on his shoulders, she pushed herself back off his lap.

She sensed his surprise and then his pleasure as she lowered herself to her knees in front of him. Pushing his thighs wide with her hands, she scooted closer.

The long blue vein that ran the length of his erection seemed to pulse in time with the music. Her pussy clenched so hard, she gasped for breath. She ached so badly for his touch. But first, she wanted to take him into her mouth and taste him, lick him and suck him to completion.

Licking her lips, she leaned forward and ran her tongue along the entire length of his penis before swirling it around the head. Liquid continued to seep from the tip and she lapped at it daintily with her tongue. Liam groaned. "You're killing me, sweetheart."

Looking up at him, she smiled before lowering her head again. This time, she opened her mouth and sucked the head inside. His fingers clenched in her hair, allowing her no escape, but she had no intention of going anywhere.

Cupping his testicles in her hand, she carefully rolled them between her fingers. She was rewarded with another groan as he thrust his hips toward her, pushing his cock deeper into her mouth. She decided right then and there that she definitely liked this. Gripping the base of his erection with her other hand, she pumped her silk-clad fingers up and down as she devoured him greedily.

He used his hold on her to guide her rhythm. With each stroke, his cock went deeper. "I want to fuck that sweet mouth and then I'm going to fuck that hot, wet pussy." His words made her hum with desire as she continued to suck his cock as deep as she could take it. He was big, so it was difficult, but she opened her mouth as wide as she could. She wanted as much of him as she could get.

"That's it, sweetheart," he crooned. "You can take more." His hips were thrusting hard, his breathing harsh as she gently squeezed his testicles. He groaned and swore, his hips jerking as he came in her mouth.

Although she'd been expecting it, she wasn't quite prepared for the hot rush of semen in her throat. She gagged once then swallowed and continued to suck until she'd drained him. Finally, at his gentle urging, she released him and leaned her head against his leg. His fingers were still tangled in her hair but when they accidentally jostled her mask, she sat up quickly and fixed it.

Liam frowned and sighed but said nothing. Cupping her face in his hand, he traced her lips with his thumb. "Thank you."

"It was my pleasure," she informed him, nipping at the tip of his thumb before sucking it into her mouth.

Liam's low rumble of laughter vibrated though her. "Enough of that, sweetheart. Now it's my turn." Standing, he zipped his jeans again, just enough to keep them from falling.

Staring down at her, his eyes were filled with promise. "Come." He held out his hand and waited for her to take it. She trusted Liam implicitly and immediately slipped her hand into his. Lending her his strength, he helped her to stand. She was grateful for his arm around her waist when she swayed on her feet. "Just a few steps," he promised.

Turning her so that she was facing him, he placed his arms around her waist and lifted her onto the side of the pool table. "Lie back." She placed her hands on the surface behind her and lowered herself until her back was against the felt-covered top.

Bending down, he wrapped his hands around her ankles and lifted them, placing them on the edge of the table. "Now, spread your legs wide."

Kelly slid her shoes along the smooth rim until her legs were as far apart as they would go. "Beautiful," he murmured as he snagged a chair and pulled it over. It aroused her to know that she was spread across the table for his pleasure and that he was seated in a chair just looking at her pussy.

"Now, I want you to keep your legs just like that." His hands were warm against her skin as he skimmed his palms up her thighs toward her sex. He positioned her hips so that her ass was perched right on the edge of the table. That spread her wide open right in front of him. She knew that she was soaked and could feel her juices dripping down her thighs but she didn't care.

His thumbs traced the folds of her pussy before spreading them. "So pink, so pretty and so fucking hot." He leaned forward until she could feel his breath on her. She cried out and thrashed her head. Her heels dug into the wooden rim, gouging deep as she struggled to keep her legs apart.

Her breasts ached so badly, she covered them with her hands. Rolling her swollen nipples between her fingers, she pinched them tight, crying out again as she did so. Liam looked up from between her spread thighs and growled. "First I'm going to eat you and then I'm going to fuck you."

"God, yes." There was nothing else she could say.

Chapter 5

Liam was in awe of the woman lying so open in front of him. She was incredible. She gave him everything he asked for, holding nothing back. Sprawled atop the pool table like some exotic sex slave, she was willing to fulfill his every desire. Although he'd come minutes before, his cock was already hard and eager to go again.

The only thing marring the encounter was her refusal to share her name but Liam shoved that thought aside. Right now, he had her right where he wanted her and he planned to enjoy it.

Her fingers were plucking hard at her distended nipples so he knew she was close to orgasm. It wouldn't take much to push her over the edge. That was fine with him—he knew she couldn't be too comfortable with the raised edge of the table digging into her lower back.

Returning his attention to the V of her thighs, he traced

the pink folds of her sex with his finger. He marveled at how wet and ready she was for him. Her arousal teased his nostrils. She even smelled hot. Her clit was swollen, the hard nub poking out from behind its hood. He lightly brushed his finger over it. Her lips parted on a breathy cry as she arched her hips toward him.

Carefully, he inserted one finger inside her, testing to see just how tight she was. Her vaginal muscles clamped down hard, gripping his finger. She was so hot and damp. He knew she could take him.

Withdrawing, he watched her as he pushed two of his long, thick fingers into her heated depths. The sensitive muscles gave way to the pressure. Liam groaned, imagining his cock buried to the hilt within her. This time when he pulled his hand back, he kept the tips of his fingers just inside the entrance. Leaning forward, he flicked her clit with his tongue at the same moment he thrust his fingers back into her pussy.

She cried out and frantically began to pump her hips. Liam hooked his free arm under one of her thighs and lifted her leg over his shoulder before clamping his hand on top of her stomach to hold her steady. He sucked her slick folds and clit as he pumped his fingers in and out of her body.

Her chest was heaving as she struggled for breath. Her hands were no longer on her breasts. Now, her fingers were tangled in his hair, tugging him closer. She cried out, she moaned, she thrashed. No woman had ever responded so honestly and completely to his touch.

He felt the change in her and knew she was close. Pulling his mouth away, he blew on her heated flesh as he plunged his fingers deep. She screamed as she came. Her hips pumped wildly and he could feel her inner muscles clamping down hard on his fingers. His cock was throbbing in time to her pussy. Next time, he would be buried inside her.

When she finally collapsed back against the table, he carefully withdrew his hand. She flinched slightly and moaned as her fingers unclenched from his hair and her arms flopped back on the table beside her. Slowly, he lifted the leg that was draped across his shoulder and let it hang over the side of the table. Then he lowered her other leg. He smiled when he saw the deep gouge in the wooden rim of the pool table and traced his thumb over it. It would forever remind him of this night and of her.

Standing, he leaned over her as he reached down and released his cock from his jeans. He pushed his hips closer to her, his erection brushing against her pussy, stroking her clit. She moaned and shivered before opening her eyes. She stared up at him, a sleepy, sated smile on her face.

"You are so damn sexy." The words were out of his mouth before he knew he meant to say them, but they were true.

"Thank you." She closed her eyes and he was afraid if he left her there too long, she might drift off to sleep. That was fine, later. When they were finished down here, he planned on carrying her upstairs to his apartment and tucking her into his king-sized bed with him right beside her. But first, he wanted to take her against the pool table.

"Hey, sweetheart." He leaned over her, placed his hands on either side of her head and traced the seam of her mouth with his tongue. Her lips parted easily and he thrust his tongue inside. He tasted the slight tartness of the wine she'd drunk earlier mixed with the musky flavor of his semen. His cock flexed in anticipation.

She reached up and cupped his face as he kissed her. Her tongue stroked his and when he withdrew, she followed, sliding her tongue into his mouth. He angled his head, deepening the kiss, never wanting it to end. Her fingers gently caressed his face before sliding into his hair. He growled deep in his throat. She was so open and giving, holding nothing back.

Her body began to move beneath his, her hips undulating, searching for him. His fingers dug into the felt of the pool table as he plunged his tongue back into her soft, seductive mouth for one final taste. Liam flexed his hips slightly, the motion causing his shaft to slide over the sensitive flesh of her pussy. It wasn't long before her thighs were clamped around his sides, squeezing him tight.

He broke away from the kiss and brushed his hair out of his eyes, wanting to see her. They both were sweaty and sticky. She looked magnificent sprawled in front of him, her eyes half-closed and her lips parted and moist. Her breasts were damp with exertion and the smell of sex wafted up from between them.

Liam had high hopes he could convince her to take a shower with him later. He took her hands in his and stepped back, pulling her into a seated position. Gripping her waist with his hands, he lifted her off the side of the table. She teetered slightly on her heels but he kept one arm around her waist to steady her.

"I want to fuck you now." Her head jerked up as he spoke

and he watched the play of emotions cross her face. He could see her blue eyes in this light and watched as the sensual haze cleared and understanding filled them.

"Oh, my. We haven't . . ." she lifted her hand and dropped it again as a small smile played around her lips. "Yet."

"No, not yet. But I want to if you're up to it." As much as it would kill him, if she was too tired, he'd carry her upstairs and tuck her into his big bed before curling up behind her. She was so tall, she'd fit him perfectly.

"I definitely want to." Her words were more of a purr as she walked her nimble fingers across his chest and flicked his flat nipples.

"Good." He turned her around to face the table before she had a chance to do anything else. Much more of those roving fingers and he'd come too quickly.

"Hey," she objected, looking back over her shoulder.

Liam gripped her hips in his hands and tugged her back toward him. "I want to take you from behind, sweetheart. I want to hear the slap of my flesh against yours. You're tall enough and filled out enough that I don't have to hold myself back."

She frowned at him. "You mean I'm big and fat."

He was appalled at her interpretation of his words. "Who the hell called you fat? You're absolutely perfect." He allowed his hands to roam over her hips before cupping her ass. "You're a real woman with curves to entice a man, to cradle him as he fucks you. With you, I can let myself go and enjoy myself, knowing that I'm bringing you pleasure as well. Do you have any idea what a gift you are?"

She blinked at him, appearing dubious.

He clamped an arm around her waist and pressed his erection against her ass. "Does that feel like I'm lying?" She wiggled her behind and he shuddered. Damn, he was close. "Sweetheart. I need you now."

"Okay," she said, turning her head back toward the table. "What do you want me to do?"

Liam's gut clenched tight. "Bend forward and place your hands against the edge of the table." He kept his arm around her waist as she bent over. Her fingers gripped the rim tight. "Now, spread your legs." Inserting his booted foot between her legs, he nudged them apart. She widened her stance.

Stepping away from her, he admired the pretty picture she made. Her breasts swung free with the bustier still wrapped around her torso. Naked from the waist down, except for her stockings and shoes, she was just begging to be fucked. Oh yeah. She was perfect. Almost.

His hand descended smartly against one fleshy globe of her ass. The smack was loud in the room and Liam realized that, somewhere along the way, the music had stopped. She jerked and gasped but didn't move. He did the same to the other side of her ass, satisfied when both cheeks flushed pink. Covering them with his hands, he gave a squeeze. "The smacks don't really hurt but they bring the blood to that area. Your ass and your pussy will be even more sensitive now."

"Do it again."

He blinked, not sure he'd heard her correctly, but she moaned and pushed her bottom back against him. Stepping back, he smacked her twice more—sharp smacks that stung more than hurt. He ruthlessly controlled his strength. He'd cut off his hand before he'd truly hurt her. This was different. This was a lover's game.

But enough was enough. Her ass was pink, her pussy was wet and his cock was screaming for release. Reaching into his pants pocket, he pulled out the condom he'd put there earlier in the evening. He tore the packet open, quickly sheathed himself and moved between her spread thighs. Positioning his erection so that just the head was inside her, he gripped her hips with his hands and surged forward, not stopping until he was buried to the hilt.

Groaning, he dropped his forehead against her back and struggled for control. With her vaginal muscles squeezing him tight, however, control was impossible to find. "I'm sorry, sweetheart." Gritting his teeth, he pulled his hips back before pushing them forward. Sweat rolled down his temple. Her inner muscles gripped him tight as he withdrew almost all the way before plunging deep again.

He was going to come. There was absolutely no way to stop it. His balls were drawn up tight against his body and he was two or three strokes away from completion. Reaching one hand around her, he found her clit with his fingers and stroked the sensitive bud, praying he could coax her into another orgasm before he exploded.

He pumped hard. Once. Twice. And then it was all over for him. His hips jerked as he emptied himself into the condom, cursing it even as he realized it was necessary. He'd wanted so badly to feel her, flesh against flesh, but even this felt unbelievably good. When he relaxed against her, he realized that she was still shaking and bucking against him. Her body was wracked with spasms as her own release shot through her. Her vaginal muscles contracted around his cock, making him groan. Damn, she felt fantastic. Eventually, the spasms lessened and finally stopped and she gave a soft sigh as she relaxed.

Liam wasn't sure how long they lay slumped against the pool table but he knew he had to move. Carefully, he withdrew his cock from her. She crumpled, legs giving out from beneath her. He caught her in his arms and carried her over to a chair, gently depositing her there. Brushing her hair away from her forehead, he smiled down at her. "I'll be back as soon as I get cleaned up. Then we'll talk."

He whistled all the way to the men's room.

Chapter 6

Kelly watched Liam walk away, mesmerized by the play of muscles in his back. She really would have liked to see his naked butt but he'd tugged up his jeans again. Once he was out of sight, it occurred to her that she was sprawled quite inelegantly in a chair.

Forcing herself to sit up, she looked down at herself. Mostly naked, she looked totally debauched. She smelled of sex and sweat and felt very sticky. The things they'd done made her want to bury her face in her hands and blush, but when they'd been doing them, they'd felt absolutely right. She had no idea how she was going to face Liam tomorrow. The only reason she wasn't in a total panic was that he had no idea who she really was. But he would soon demand answers.

That thought galvanized her into action. Surging to her feet, she hurried over to the pool table and plucked her skirt off the floor. Shaking out the layers of fabric, she stepped into the skirt and quickly zipped and buttoned it. She didn't think it was possible for her to run in heels but she did so now, quickly racing back to the bar. Yanking up the ends of the bustier, she shoved her breasts back inside. Grabbing her coat, she ran for the door. She didn't look back, afraid if she did, she wouldn't be able to leave.

She was almost to the door when she heard the pounding of boots behind her. Fumbling for the locks, she almost had the door open when his large hand slammed against the door with a bang. Kelly jumped but refused to turn around.

"Going somewhere?" The tone of his voice suggested that he was mildly interested in her reply but Kelly knew the truth. Liam was furious.

"It's time for me to go home." She felt his hands on her shoulders and she hunched forward. He sighed and withdrew. She missed his touch the moment it was gone.

"So you were just going to run out and never tell me your name." Kelly forced herself to turn around and face him. He looked hurt and angry.

Gently, she cupped his face in her hand. "I never meant to hurt you."

"Then what did you mean to do?" She could tell by the look in his eyes that he honestly wanted to know.

"I wanted to fulfill a fantasy."

"And this was the only way you could do it?" His voice was softer now and his hand covered hers, holding it against his face.

Closing her eyes against the pain, she took a deep breath and opened them again. "Yes. Disguised in a costume, I can masquerade as something I'm really not."

"And what's that?" Liam rested his other hand against the small of her back, subtly urging her closer.

"A sexy, desirable woman who can seduce the man of her dreams."

He frowned at her. "You are sexy and desirable."

Kelly shook her head. "It's just the costume, the masquerade, this special night. In the light of day, I'm ordinary and plain. Just like the decorations." Lifting a hand, she motioned to the room. "They looked so fantastic tonight but when your staff comes in to clean up tomorrow morning, they'll just look tacky and worn."

"So what we just shared wasn't special?" His words were laced with anger and what she thought might be pain. This wasn't supposed to happen. She only wanted to grab one night of happiness for herself, not hurt him.

"No." She shook her head in denial. "What we shared was more special than you'll ever possibly know. But it's not real. It's only for this one night." Drawing on every ounce of strength she possessed, she pulled away, both thankful and hurt when he just dropped his arms and let her go.

She gave him a shaky smile and turned back to the door. She had the locks undone and her fingers wrapped around the handle when he spoke. "You really think I didn't know it was you, Kelly?"

Her suddenly nerveless fingers fell from the door as she turned back toward him. With his arms crossed over his chest, his legs spread wide and his long hair tousled, he looked more like a pirate than ever. "How did you know? How could you know?"

"How?" He leaned toward her, crowding her back against

the door before placing a hand on either side of her head, effectively caging her within his arms. "I've been watching you for a year now, sweetheart."

She shook her head, unable to believe his words.

"Oh yes," he continued. "I know every curve of your luscious body. I know that you laugh at the customers' stupid jokes and that you're kind to everyone you meet, without exception. I know you love baseball but hate football." He gave her a loving smile. "That's a serious flaw but I can overlook that." His dark eyes continued to search her face. "I know your favorite perfume is some exotic, flowery concoction that's both subtle and wild at the same time and that it makes my cock throb. You have a weakness for expensive dark chocolate. I know you prefer white wine to red and that you'd rather stay home and curl up with a good book or a movie than party all night long."

Her head was spinning but he wasn't finished yet. "I know that I've wanted you from the moment you came to work for me but you were an employee and I never get involved with my staff. If you'd ever shown a bit of interest in me, I'd have been tempted to fire you just so I could fuck you. But you never gave me any encouragement and you're too damned good a friend and waitress to lose."

"I didn't know." Kelly knew that Liam would never have fired her because of his attraction but that it was his way of letting her know just how badly he wanted her. It was strange to have her perceptions changed so quickly. Had she been wearing blinders for the past year or was he as good at hiding his feelings as she was? No matter, the truth was out now and there was no going back. She tentatively placed her hand on his chest, almost afraid to touch him now. She could feel the heavy thud of his heart against her palm.

"Of course you didn't know. I wasn't going to jump you in a back room if you weren't interested. And it's obvious you have no idea just how damn sexy you are even when you're wearing your hair pulled back tight with your white blouse buttoned to your chin."

Kelly could hardly keep up with Liam. "You think I'm sexy?"

"You are walking, talking sex." He smiled at her. "All those buttons just make a man want to unbutton them and discover the treasures you keep hidden underneath." His smile died. "I've bared my soul. What about you? How do you feel?"

"Oh, Liam." She flung her arms around his waist and buried her face against his chest. "I've wanted you from the moment I saw you and I've loved you for months. I just could never imagine that you'd feel the same way."

She felt him stiffen the second the word "love" came from her mouth but it was too late to call it back now. It was time to lay all her cards on the table. Leaning back against the door, she stared him straight in the eyes. "I love you, Liam Brannigan. What do you have to say about that?"

His face gave no indication of his emotions and he paused for so long that Kelly began to worry. But then a slow smile covered his face. "I'd say that I'm a very lucky man." He brushed her cheek with his fingers. "And that I love you too."

Reaching up, he hooked his fingers in the strap of her mask, slowly lifting it from her face. "It's time to unmask the mystery lady to reveal the woman I love and want in my life."

Kelly blinked up at him, glad to finally have the hot

mask off her face. She wasn't afraid to face him any longer, knowing that he saw her as she truly was and loved her for it. Liam swept her up into his arms and swung her around in a circle. Laughing, she gripped his neck tight for support. When he finally stopped, her head was still spinning but she was smiling.

"Lock the door again, sweetheart." Liam held her next to the door while she turned all the locks. With her still in his arms, he carried her from table to table around the room until the few remaining candles that hadn't burned themselves out were extinguished. Then he headed toward the set of stairs that led to his apartment.

Kelly toyed with a lock of his hair. "So," she began. "Does this mean I'm fired?"

He was halfway up the stairs before he answered her. "Well, it does pose a problem. But you're too good a waitress to lose. All the customers love you." When he gained the top of the stairs, he walked toward his apartment door and opened it. Stepping inside, he shut it with his hip and leaned against it. "I guess I only have one solution."

"What's that?" His blue eyes held a warmth that curled her toes.

"I guess you'll just have to marry me."

Kelly smiled up at him, knowing he'd just offered her everything she'd ever wanted. "I guess I will."

He carried her down the hall and into the master bedroom, kicking the door closed behind him.

Sinderella

JAN SPRINGER

Chapter 1

Ella's heart raced as she lay bound and naked on the gynecologist's examination table. A fine sheen of perspiration laced her skin. Her hips undulated as Roarke fucked her with the dual vibrator. Sucking sounds of her soaked pussy clutching the sex toy just about drove her mad. Her well-lubed ass burned with pleasure-pain every time he thrust into her and the erotic way the stimulator slid softly over her aching clitoris had her pulling against her bound legs and wrists as she tried to escape the incredible sexual tension.

The rhythmic motions made her body hum, pulse, ache for release.

He'd kept her on the edge of a climax for so long she could barely think straight.

"I've wanted to do this to you since the first day I met you,

Ella." His deep voice smoothed over her flushed skin like a jolt of lightning.

"You want more, Ella?"

Excitement flared like a firecracker. Her body trembled.

She could barely see him through the sexual haze. Could hardly see his sparkling, lust-filled green eyes or the sexy smile he reserved only for her.

Oh, God!

She wanted his long, thick cock inside her, not the freaking vibrator!

"I want you," she pleaded hoarsely, and thrashed her head back and forth. She needed to come so bad. Needed release or she would simply go mad with desire.

"Please, Roarke, please make love to me. Please fuck me," she whimpered.

"And so you shall have me, Ella," he said hoarsely. His face twisted with sexual hunger. "You shall have my big cock deep inside your tight little pussy—"

"Good morning, sorry I'm late," Dr. Roarke Stephenson's deep, masculine voice slammed into Dr. Ella Cinder's fantasy like a sensual punch, making her suck in her breath and spill her coffee onto the elaborate oak conference table.

"Christ, Ella! You're such a damn loser!" Her stepmother's harsh whisper made her flinch and Ella quickly threw a pile of napkins over the puddle of steaming coffee.

Her face flamed as her two stepsisters, Drs. Wanda and Manda Cinder elbowed each other gleefully and chuckled snidely beside her.

Bitches! Ella thought as she pushed against the bridge

of her old black-framed glasses in order to keep them from falling off her nose while she wiped at the steaming coffee. From the corner of her eye she spied the man of her frequent sexual fantasies stroll into the room.

He scowled at her stepmother, obviously overhearing her rude remark, but thankfully, he said nothing. Roarke was still relatively new and she didn't want him getting into trouble on her account.

When he passed by, his delicious male scent slammed into her with such a wicked force her senses spiraled into sexual awareness mode.

Oh, God! He always looked so damned sexy. He wore the traditional white lab coat fully opened, revealing a light green shirt that stretched across his big chest as well as a pair of tight jeans that cradled his awesomely huge bulge. With shoulder-length black hair pulled back in a tight ponytail and a shadowy stubble covering his strong jaw, he looked more like a dangerous bad boy than a prestigious gynecologist.

He sat down beside her and she noted his lust-sparkling gaze slide over her in one hot wave making her entire body tighten with need.

Her self-control, or at least what was left of it, crumbled as visions of her most recent fantasy invaded her thoughts again. Their naked bodies fused. The scent of their sex hanging heavy in the air. His long, thick cock pushing deep inside her wet, hungry vagina.

Her pussy creamed in reaction.

Oh, God! She had to stop fantasizing about the sexy doctor. She had a bad habit of daydreaming about him whenever she felt overworked and tired . . . which was pretty much all the time. Overworked because she accepted twice the number of patients than any other doctor in the hospital did at the same wage they got, and tired because of her deliciously naughty nighttime activities. Activities that made her fantasize about Roarke day and night.

Was it any wonder whenever he came near her she felt so nervous and flustered she became all thumbs?

The last thing she wanted to do was to appear incompetent in front of her fellow gynecologists. Especially when she needed them for the occasional problem cases she snuck into the consultation pile, just like the one she'd boldly plopped onto the pile today. She didn't want her patient to suffer any longer, and had decided to bite the bullet and seek the second signature required as per Cinder policy for giving medication without awaiting the lab results to confirm her suspicions.

"You really should cut down on all that daydreaming, Ella." Her anorexic stepsister Manda rolled her eyes with disgust. Then she scrunched her thin lips in an unattractive grimace as she looked at the pile of donuts set on a crystal plate in the middle of the conference table.

"It's not her daydreaming. The klutz simply drinks too much coffee," her other stepsister Wanda chuckled as she heaved her overweight frame out of her chair and picked up her fourth chocolate-dipped donut.

Ella sighed wearily as their comments needled into her heart. By now she should be immune to their rudeness. Yet she wasn't. Compliments of her oversensitive nature, she supposed.

What in the world had she done to deserve such a horrid stepfamily anyway?

"Doctors, please. Let's not show our immaturity so early in the morning," Roarke grumbled as he poured some coffee and grabbed a donut. To Ella's surprise he winked at her.

Oh sweet mercy! Roarke winked at her, and she was gushing back at him like a silly schoolgirl.

"Oh for crying out loud, Ella. Hurry up and clean the mess so we can get on with today's caseload. We're already ten minutes behind schedule," her stepmother huffed. Disgust flashed on her wrinkled face and her three chins wobbled as she also grabbed herself a donut.

Ella bit back a sharp retort. She wished she could just tell them where to stick their donuts and their snide remarks. One of these days she would do just that. Not today though. Today she needed their help.

"So tell me about this latest problem case you're working on? This girl named China Smith," Roarke suddenly asked. She hadn't even noticed he'd started reading the file of her problem case.

Ella stopped wiping the table. Ignoring the irritated looks of her stepsisters and stepmother, she relished the familiar pounding of adrenaline that roared through her system. This time it wasn't the usual sexual energy she felt whenever she thought of Roarke, but the energy of living on the edge with these complicated pregnancy cases she had a tendency of taking on.

"Her symptoms include a rash, a stiff neck, blood in her mouth, seizures, to name a few," Ella replied in a rush, hoping her stepfamily wouldn't interfere just yet with their embarrassing protests. "I've done the appropriate tests to rule out stomach cancer, sepsis, meningitis, checked for intracranial bleeding—"

"What do you know about her personal life?" he asked softly. His gaze held hers and Ella took yet another deep breath to steady her nerves. Was that concern in Roarke's eyes? Or was he deliberately prodding her for more information so her stepfamily could gloat when they shot her down. No, he wouldn't intentionally hurt her.

Although there was nothing she could put her finger on, she sensed there was a gentle side to this confident man. A side he kept well hidden. Up until now he'd seemed to fit in at the hospital quite nicely, thinking only in dollars and cents and taking in wealthy clients who would benefit the hospital. Perfect Cinder material, her stepmother had cooed after they'd interviewed him several months ago. Perfect husband material, her stepsisters had whispered.

Ella had been smitten with him too. Wishing and dreaming that she would one day have this handsome, confident, rich doctor for her very own. Unfortunately her dreams and wishes had died a cruel death when she'd seen the photograph of him and his fiancée in his office shortly after he'd been hired.

Over the months he'd appeared quite the professional with her. Those heated looks she caught him throwing her way were probably just her imagination, but they'd ignited erotic fantasies that just kept on coming.

"She's thirteen," Ella admitted. "About four months pregnant, a prostitute, no prenatal care and she desperately wants to keep the baby."

Her anxiety mounted as the others mumbled their disgust. Thankfully she managed to keep her attention focused on Roarke, who merely nodded and kept reading.

A moment later he cocked an eyebrow as he shuffled through yet another report she'd put in the pregnant girl's file. "Her blood looks like it's been whipped through a mixer. Her pregnancy could have thrown her hormones totally out of control. Have you checked for TTP?"

TTP or Thrombotic Thrombocytopenic Purpura. It was a rare condition that she'd only considered when the other lab results had come back clean. TTP could be deadly to both the baby and mother as it turned a pregnant woman's body against her and caused a host of problems from seemingly innocent rashes to awful seizures.

"I'm waiting on those test results now." She wanted to ask him for the required signature right then but, despite her impatience, she figured it was best to wait until he'd read the entire file on the off chance she'd missed something.

Apprehension mounted as he said nothing and shifted through more of the contents of the folder.

Ella inhaled slowly, trying to keep a tight grip on her frustration about her young, sick patient. She'd found the pregnant girl huddled on her assigned parking spot in the elaborate Cinder hospital's underground parking lot yesterday morning. How she'd gotten past security, Ella had no idea, but the girl's dark brown eyes had pleaded for her help. She'd said she'd heard of Ella's sympathetic nature and about Cinder's specialized hospital through a mutual friend. Had told Ella she sensed there was something terribly wrong with her pregnancy. Had begged for her to save her baby. A moment later the girl had gone into convulsions right then and there.

"I don't know why you two are even bothering to discuss her case," Manda snapped as she licked chocolate icing from her fingers. "As you said the slut is homeless and a prostitute. She's scandalous for our hospital. If anyone gets wind of her being here, it could ruin our reputation."

"Her pimp probably holds her purse strings," her other stepsister chimed in. "He won't pay to fix her up. He'll simply get another hooker to take her place."

"She's simply a waste of our time," her stepmother cooed. "Let's please move onto the next case."

The familiar burst of anger erupted inside Ella at their cavalier attitude toward a young woman's life. But she kept her mouth shut and her emotions of disgust and anger well hidden. She'd learned early in life that arguing with her stepfamily was unproductive.

"Let's work like the team we're supposed to be, shall we? Isn't that one of the reasons I was hired for? To shape us all into a team?" Roarke said abruptly. Without waiting for an answer he continued, "This young girl is good promo for Cinder Hospital."

Was that a tinge of anger she detected in his voice? Was it aimed at her? Or the rude, unprofessional behavior of the others?

"How is a homeless, pregnant prostitute good for us?" her stepmother broke in. Her perfectly arched tattooed eyebrows rose in curiosity at Roarke's promo comment.

"We can leak word to the medical press. Tell them that due to the quick thinking of Cinder's hospital staff, a pregnant woman's rare condition was quickly treated and her life was saved. It will give Cinder free promo in the headlines. Other hospitals and doctors will seek us out with their problem pregnancy cases."

"Yeah and those cases won't be able to pay just like this one," Wanda grumbled.

"That's not the point," Roarke said rather coolly.

Internally Ella cheered him on as he settled casually back against his seat and threw her stepsister a disarming smile. "Our clients will realize we're sympathetic toward the less fortunate. It'll make us appear more . . . human."

Ouch!

Her stepmother and stepsisters all frowned. It was obvious they didn't like what Roarke was saying. They only took on cases from rich, snobby people who could pay their exorbitant professional fees. Due to the increase in rates, just to subsidize their high living now that her stepfamily had finally drained her father's estate, business for Cinder Gynecological Hospital had taken a downward turn.

"I think what Roarke also means," Ella came to his rescue, taking advantage of the thread he'd created, "is that we can also leak word to the general public via the newspapers. I know a couple of reporters," she lied. "I can release word we saved the life of a very young pregnant girl. It will garner sympathy in a lot of mothers' eyes. Mothers who have daughters of their own. Mothers who will remember us when their daughters get pregnant and run into medical problems. We'll be discreet about what hits the newspapers. We'll feed them only the appropriate information about a problem case that was quickly solved due to the quick thinking of the Cinder

Team. TTP is rare. Most hospitals don't even test for it until they rule out a cause for each symptom as it appears. Those tests can be torturous on the patient. We'll mention we're private. That will eliminate the needy and low-income cases." Of course she'd forget to mention the private part. As far as she was concerned, she would accept any patient who had a complication in her pregnancy, poor or rich. Payments could be worked out afterward. "We'll make sure this case hits the medical journals also. As Roarke mentioned, other non-private hospitals will refer their pregnancy problem cases to us especially if they are overcrowded, hence more business for us. I'm sure with Cinder agreeing to pay for the girl's hospital stay and her medication, it's a small cost for all the future business she'll be bringing in."

"Exactly." Roarke slammed the file onto the table and stood. "Now let's get our asses in gear. I don't want to wait for the test results to come in. Let's get her on the meds before it's too late. Ella, she's your client. You tell her what's happening."

"I'll tell her."

"I can see you've already got the requisition form signed. I'll sign it too as your backup and get it over to the nurses' station. They can start administering right away," he said.

Ella nodded, suddenly feeling a burden lift off her. It felt good having someone else on her side for a change. Very good. However, now wasn't the time to relish in her relief. She had a patient to see.

"Just one moment!" her stepmother snapped as Ella stood. "You stay right there, Ella. Mandy you call an ambulance to get Ella's slut out of here. We cannot go against protocol and administer drugs to someone like that without the proper lab results. We could be sued if Ella is wrong."

"Then they'll have to sue me too," Roarke snapped with apparent irritation.

Ella broke in. "According to Cinder protocol, if two doctors decide it is in the best interest of the patient to administer drugs without having the lab results yet, all that is needed is a second signature. I have that signature from Dr. Stephenson. You wouldn't want to go against our own protocol would you, Stepmother?"

Ella didn't wait for her answer. Instead she forced herself not to smile at the furious looks plastered across her Stepmother and stepsisters' faces as she followed Roarke out the door.

Later that day Roarke swore like a son of a bitch when he hopped into his car and maneuvered out of Cinder's parking lot. As the months passed it became increasingly difficult to remember why he'd taken on this job with the prestigious Cinder Hospital. Lately he'd had to constantly remind himself that the fantastic pay he received from this establishment would keep his dream alive. A dream it seemed he'd been working his ass off for much too long.

Today's case of China had really hit home. Too bad he'd had yesterday off or he would have been able to help the girl earlier. Ella was an excellent doctor. Unfortunately, she'd never had the support she needed from her step-broads and understandably kept her Good Samaritan cases well hidden. This case had been a close call. Too close. If Ella had waited for the test results, the baby and mother could have been irreparably harmed. Or died.

He'd been stunned to say the least when he'd found the homeless girl's file sitting right up at the top of today's consultation pile. Either Ella was finally getting herself some balls and standing up for herself and her patients, or she'd just been desperate in this case.

"Fuck!" He slammed his fists against the steering wheel, feeling the gut-wrenching frustration turning his belly into a queasy knot. Why the hell hadn't she called him at home about this case?

Hell! He knew the answer to that. Days off at Cinder were "do not disturb the doctor's day off." No on calls and no midnight surgeries. Just shitty nine-to-five shifts. But that's one of the things that had attracted him to this hospital in the first place. Fantastic pay and evenings free to help take care of his girls.

By day he gave breast and pelvic exams to rich, horny women who winked and flirted with him as they placed their legs into stirrups and acted as if having a metal probe slip into their vaginas was akin to him fucking them.

Unfortunately for him, the only pussy he wanted to fuck belonged to sweet, klutzy Ella.

Her shyness and refusal to stand up for herself irritated him and attracted him at the same time. Overall she seemed a gentle woman, but on days like today she proved she had streaks of boldness. To further his irritation, she continued to drown her innocent-looking baby blue eyes behind sexy black-rimmed glasses that simply made his hormones go haywire every time he saw them.

Roarke frowned. Maybe he had a glasses fetish or something? No, it couldn't be that. Every time he saw her, he became transfixed by her compelling beauty. The lack of makeup allowed her skin tone to glow and her natural beauty to shine. Her cheeks always seemed flushed, and although her hair was a mousy brown and short and spiky, sometimes windblown, it gave him the impression she'd just tumbled out of bed after a night of mind-blowing sex with some lucky guy.

He'd done some discreet investigating and discovered from the staff as well as some patients that Ella didn't seem to date and kept mostly to herself.

Too bad he'd decided she was off-limits due to the fact she was a part owner of the hospital. Although she never acted like she was the daughter of the man who'd started the private hospital, he'd decided long ago in his career it was safest to never mix business with pleasure. Or he'd be pursuing Ella with a passion. There was nothing more he wanted than to have her naked and bound. His engorged cock driving shrieks of delight from her flushed body.

Roarke blew out a tense breath. Right now he couldn't think about sexy Ella or he'd end up masturbating right there in the car. He needed to keep his focus on why he'd taken this job and why he'd told everyone at work the big white lie that he had a fiancée.

Truth was, he rarely had the time to date. Speaking of time, he glanced at his watch.

Shit!

If he didn't get home, shower and change, he'd be late for the private adult play of Sinderella showing at his colleague

Merck's house. The man was an asshole but he was also an old coworker who knew a lot of important people in the medical profession. Burning bridges with Merck was not an option if he intended to continue climbing up the ladder. Merck was a bit of a ladies' man so he wasn't surprised when the older man had mentioned he was hosting an adult play in his home tonight. Roarke had been invited on several previous occasions but he'd always been busy. Tonight however, he'd decided it was time to cut loose. Merck had also said the play would blow Roarke's mind.

Right then he needed a damn good distraction before his own mind exploded with the anger he felt toward the Cinder bitches' casual attitude regarding the less fortunate as well as their mistreatment of Ella. Usually he kept his annoyance well hidden. If he didn't, he'd surely get fired when he told his employers exactly what he thought about their rudeness. The three of them acted so fucking immature that sometimes he simply wanted to tell them to drop dead or to shove their jobs up where the sun doesn't shine.

But every time he saw Ella he had the totally opposite reaction. He wanted to take her into his arms, kiss her and do so many naughty things to her. Naughty things that would make her blush up a storm.

Today he couldn't help but allow her to see a bit of his soft side, and damned if it hadn't given her a boost. He'd felt quite smug at having her follow him out instead of staying behind as her stepmother had ordered.

Ironic that he was going to see this private Sinderella play. Kind of reminded him of Ella and her mean stepmother and nasty stepsisters.

Gripping the steering wheel tighter, he pressed harder on the gas pedal.

Since before meeting Ella he'd never had any trouble unwinding with some no-holds-barred casual sex with his women friends. Now however, the only person he wanted to have sex with was his klutzy coworker.

Since that was out of the question, he'd just have to force himself to relax tonight. To forget the young, pregnant prostitute who'd reminded him so much of his own young mother and to shove out of his mind the sexy, shy doctor who quite literally had him by the balls.

Chapter 2

Ella stood at the back door of Merck Manor, a dark brooding castle-like building nestled on seven acres of lush fields in upstate New York. She stifled a sob before shoving yet another tissue beneath the silver mask she wore for her secret performances as Sinderella.

Call her sexually twisted or perhaps she was just shy, but the mask allowed her to participate in many naughty adult scenes.

Sinderella. Her invention. Her naughty secret. Her creative release from reality.

Performing always calmed her down. It was the only time she felt alive and free and separate from her stressful life. Of course keeping her face hidden behind a mask helped. If the people she performed in front of knew her true identity, she'd never be able to do the naughty things she did in front of them. It was because of the luscious sex acts she and her masked troupe performed in the privacy of other people's homes that made Sinderella such a wild success.

If ever there were a night she needed to escape the pressures of her day job, tonight was the night. After seeing China's quick recovery due to the meds Roarke had cosigned, she'd been bawling like a baby. She did that when one of her really sick patients started to get better. She couldn't help being emotional. Had always been that way especially because of her innate ability of putting herself in each of her patient's shoes.

This time the tissue came away damp instead of soaked. Well, at least she was improving.

Running a hand through the shoulder-length, luscious blond curls of the wig she wore, she looked down at herself and admired the skintight black outfit peeking out from her open spring jacket. The sexy clothing hugged her every sensual curve and allowed a generous amount of skin to show. The halter top gave quite a revealing view of her creamy breasts and the thong that barely covered her pussy would allow her audience to view her naked ass.

To keep herself in shape for her secret performances, she worked out for a couple of hours every morning in the privacy of her apartment. Aerobics, weight bearing exercises, the treadmill, rowing machine and daily jogging at a nearby park. She did all of it to keep her abs perfectly toned and her body perfectly curvy. Not to mention the exercise helped to wake her up from her naughty, late-night activities.

Excitement began to push away her tears and she rapped on the back door.

She had to wait only a few seconds and the door swung

open. Caprice, the motherly woman who Ella had hired to play her fairy godmother in the play, stood there worrying her lower lip.

Uh-oh, when Caprice bit her lower lip it meant trouble. She wasn't wrong.

"Dammit, Sin. Where the hell have you been? The audience is here and they're getting nervous. We were supposed to open fifteen minutes ago," she whispered as she quickly ushered Ella in the back door and down the dimly lit hall of Merck Mansion.

"And Prince Charming never showed either," she added.

"Shit!" Trouble. Big-time.

This just wasn't her day, was it? First she'd had to ask for help with her case and now her freaking Prince Charming had dumped her.

"The next time you hear from him tell him he's fired. We'll start looking for another prince first thing in the morning."

Caprice nodded.

They slid into the room where the rest of the small group had gathered in their colorful, sexy outfits. The instant they saw Ella they stopped talking and waited eagerly for further instructions from her.

God, she loved being the boss. The power made her feel strong and confident—something she never felt in the medical world where her stepsisters and stepmother always managed to make her feel like a clumsy idiot.

"The performance is still on," Ella reassured the small group as she slipped off her jacket and shoes and put on her black dance slippers.

"I've already mentioned to Merck what the problem is, he

said he'd be more than happy to play the prince," the petite, white-haired elderly woman who played Prince Charming's mother said innocently.

I'm sure he did.

Merck had a crush on her. Well, maybe a crush was too gentle a word. He wanted her in his bed and that's the last place she ever wanted to be.

"I'll scan the crowd for a prince before any decisions are made." At least that way she'd have some control over what happened tonight. In order for the play to work she needed someone she was halfway attracted to.

Someone like Roarke.

Just thinking about him made her pussy clench wickedly and cream with liquid heat.

Oh yeah, Roarke would be her perfect Prince Charming. But now was not the time to start fantasizing.

Ella clapped her hands. "Okay everyone. Don't worry. We'll find a prince. As always, let's give them hell tonight!"

The group cheered.

"You guys are the best," Ella complimented her smiling troupe.

She nodded to Caprice who quickly tied the traditional peasant kerchief over Ella's wig and smudged her cheeks lightly with black soot to give the effect of a woman who spent most of her time cleaning. Then she led Ella from the room. A moment later she stood outside the door of the room they'd be performing in.

The first act she'd be alone doing a sensual dance while cleaning out the fireplace. She'd also be singing one of the songs she'd learned by heart when she'd been a kid and watched various Cinderella plays over and over again. Of course, she'd made her own adjustments to the tunes, turning it into an adult play her group performed secretly for private audiences. Ella's take of the money went anonymously toward several local charities.

Tonight wasn't the first night she'd have to pick a man from the audience to play her prince. For some reason the part of Prince Charming was the one most often recast . . . usually because after the show the prince wanted the play to continue . . . in the bedroom. She had no patience for such unprofessionalism. She considered Sinderella a tasteful, professional, adult spin-off of Cinderella from which, according to the rumors, she'd heard it had been originally invented for adults long before it had been reinvented for children.

Her Sinderella version was a serious, lucrative business and there was no time to play to a man's ego or his aroused cock after the show. It was up to him and not her to get himself relief.

Gosh, she still couldn't believe she did this erotic stuff. If her stepmother and stepsisters found out about her secret life, they'd die right on the spot.

Ella smiled. Wouldn't that be a lovely thing to happen? To see their shocked expressions if they ever discovered their loser, klutzy Ella wasn't as much of a loser or as clumsy as they always teased her about being.

Music drifted from the room. It was her cue.

Swallowing back a last blast of stage fright, she forced herself to glide into the dimly lit room. As she appeared, shocked gasps rang out. A maddening applause quickly followed. The warm welcome washed a sizzling rush through her almost nude body and she couldn't help but be pleased at the way her troupe had decorated the performance room.

Ordinarily Merck used it as his library. On presentation nights, it became Sinderella's living room. Pine beams laced the white stuccoed ceiling and a cheerful fire crackled inside the fieldstone fireplace. Pulled in front of the hearth sat a lone New York ladder-back chair. It would come in very handy in just a few moments.

Grabbing her feather duster with the dildo-shaped handle from the fireplace hearth, she began to dust the furniture and sang her sad tale to the audience of mostly men.

She was Sinderella. Lost in a world of servitude. Her father had married a nasty woman who had two awful daughters. He'd died and her stepfamily had made her their servant. Their slave, who cleaned the chimneys and dusted the house while she fantasized about being rescued from her dismal life.

The song always gripped her heart. It was a song of fantasies. Fantasies of who she wanted to be. Of pretending she was a beautiful princess and had fallen in love with a well-hung prince who would cherish her and make love to her every day—it made her feel sorry because she knew in reality romance would never happen to her. She was thirty and had never been on a date. Why start now? Sinderella was her sex life and she enjoyed it immensely, even if it wasn't normal behavior for a woman.

While she performed, dancing about with her feather duster, she scanned the excited faces of the numerous male members in her search for a Prince Charming. No one captured her interest tonight.

Frustration began to claw at her belly at the thought of giving in to Merck and allowing him to be her prince. Merck enjoyed tormenting her by dropping hints that if she wanted him to continue to throw private showings for Sinderella, she would have to sleep with him.

He was a millionaire heart surgeon and by far Sinderella's greatest sponsor. She needed to consider his threat and either do as he asked or tell him to shove his request right up his ass.

She leaned heavily to the latter.

Denying Merck would put a dent into the pocketbook of the charities she anonymously donated her share of the Sinderella performances to, but she did have her principles.

Suddenly from the corner of her eye she noticed a door opening at the other end of the room.

A latecomer.

Her breath caught as she spied the silhouette standing in the open doorway. The play of light and shadow hit his face in just the right way, illuminating his profile. Blunt cheekbones, straight nose and sharp angles that made her heart kick-start.

Roarke?

She almost faltered in her song but managed to keep on track, her pulses picking up speed as he hunched into the shadows. He moved with the confidence of a man on the prowl. Just like Roarke.

Oh, God! It couldn't be him, could it?

She noted the extra-wide shoulders, his tall figure. The dark hair pulled back off his face as if he wore a ponytail . . .

Just like Roarke.

Her body tightened with awareness. Carnal sensations bombarded her most intimate parts. She could literally feel her nipples elongate. Her breasts wanted to be touched, to be cupped, to be held. Her pussy sizzled to life and she ached to be filled by this newcomer's cock.

She almost faltered again as the wicked assault heated her with exquisite want. Almost dropped her feather duster as she slid onto the chair they'd set beside the fireplace just for her.

Angling herself so the newcomer would have the best view, she artfully spread her legs wide, capturing his full attention. Even in the darkness she felt his hot stare upon her flesh as she teasingly guided the dildo-shaped handle of her feather duster up along her thighs, getting closer and closer to her thong.

She'd known right from the beginning when she'd first conceived the idea for this show that her sexual prowess became heightened when people watched her doing intimate things to herself. Without her face being hidden though, she would never have the nerve to be so bold. Would have been much too embarrassed as to what she was doing in front of all these eager patrons.

She continued to sing about her fantasies of a well-hung man coming to her rescue while her free hand tugged at the string holding her thong in place.

The thin garment fell away. Warm air breathed against her pulsing flesh, revealing to all her nude pussy.

Women gasped and men leaned forward in their seats to get a closer look. Sinderella held the newcomer's fierce gaze.

Using the tip of the dildo, she split her pulsing pussy lips and gently rubbed her engorged clitoris. Within seconds she felt the familiar stirrings of arousal and couldn't help the moan from escaping her mouth as she dipped inside her entrance, stretching her vagina as she collected the juices quickly accumulating.

Tension mounted inside her as she slid the now lubed dildo over and over her aching clitoris. Her thighs tightened. She forced herself to keep her legs apart, giving the stranger a prelude of things to come should he accept her offer to be her Prince Charming tonight.

Her breaths grew quicker. Her breasts strained against the tight halter.

With her free hand nestled over a clothed breast she pinched her nipple, gasping at the pleasure-burn.

She continued to rub her sensitive, wet clit. Need grabbed ahold of her cunt. Her body began to ache. Involuntarily her hips arched and gyrated, the fierce arousal rising quickly now.

This act was only one of the erotic sights that made her play famous. She never faked an orgasm during this scene. She knew the tender parts of her body well. Loved touching herself. Arousing herself in the privacy of her own bedroom as well as in front of her captive audience. Tonight especially she enjoyed fucking herself in front of this dark stranger who looked too familiar.

The newcomer, unlike the other men who leaned forward in their chairs, remained seated in a leisurely, relaxed pose. She sensed he was fully enjoying what she was doing to herself. Could almost imagine his scorching grin. A grin that would look just like Roarke's.

Her breathing stalled. At the thought of this stranger actually being Roarke, the man she'd been fantasizing about for so long, she moved the dildo quicker against her swollen clit, dipping harder into her vagina gathering more of her juices.

Her body sizzled, ached to be touched, to be held by this newcomer. She blew out a breath and almost faltered.

She'd tell Caprice to seek him out when she finished this scene. To ask him if he'd mind being her Prince Charming to-night.

Clenching her teeth, she bit back yet another moan. Her breath halted as the beautiful sensations whipped through her. She shuddered.

Plunging the dildo faster and faster in and out of her pussy, she keened and hissed as the inferno spread. Grinding her hips against the dildo, she finally allowed herself to lose control.

Just before she closed her eyes to welcome her orgasm, she took immense delight when the stranger shifted uneasily in his chair and leaned just a wee bit closer.

Oh yes! Come closer. Come closer.

Ella closed her eyes and groaned out her hot release.

Roarke couldn't keep his eyes off the luscious, curvy blonde. She'd been dancing erotically when he'd arrived, not to mention barely clothed. The carnal sight caught him totally off guard. He'd stood in the doorway transfixed by her beauty. Totally in lust as he'd watched her every movement sensually orchestrated, her voice so soft and familiar it slid over his flesh like a seductive lover's song.

Everything about her called to him. Made his cock shoot into alert mode. Her full, kissable lips reminded him of Ella's. Her long, smooth, feminine legs begged to clasp around his hips. And he found himself wanting to buck his engorged cock in and out of her slit until she cried out in pleasure.

Beneath her skintight halter he easily made out the two lusciously curved mounds that pushed against the slinky, black lattice cloth. His hands itched to cup her breasts. To feel their weight. His fingers ached to pinch what he could tell were unusually large nipples.

When she'd sat on the chair and spread her legs, her fiery gaze had captured his. He'd been amused at the feather duster turning into a dildo. But when the thong gave way to a deliciously nude pussy, her inner thighs glistening with wetness, her labia plump and her clit red and engorged, Roarke's cock had hardened and lengthened like a thick piece of steel.

His reaction surprised him. Lately he'd only been reacting this violently whenever he got near Ella. From what he could make out about this woman, she did look similar to his klutzy colleague. Maybe that's why he was so captivated with this woman.

He almost laughed out loud at that thought.

Ella and Sinderella were total opposites, but there was something attractive about this woman, just as there was something attractive about Ella.

However Ella was off-limits. This woman wasn't. He focused his attention on Sinderella.

Every inch of her oozed sexuality. Every soft curve delighted his imagination. Her luscious clit looked engorged and ruby red. Ready for his lips to suck and taste and tease.

His mouth watered at the delicious thought.

She was aroused.

Big-time.

"So? What do you think about Sinderella?" Merck nudged him out of his hot trance. For a moment Roarke wanted to tell his colleague to fuck off so he could enjoy the show. But it wouldn't do to antagonize Merck. He'd have the information Roarke would need about this mysterious woman.

"Who is she? I'd like to meet her after the show." No use beating around the bush.

"That's the beauty of it. No one knows her true identity. The entire troupe performs with masks and they only accept cash in payment so there's no paper trail. They all leave in separate cars and, from what I've heard, most of the actors don't know her real identity. Maybe you'll get lucky."

Damned right he'd get lucky, Roarke thought as he settled back against his seat to enjoy the show. He couldn't wait to find out more about this mystery woman who hid her face behind that mask. Most of all he needed to find out why she sounded so damned familiar.

Ella's pulses blasted heat through her veins as she awaited her next scene. She'd sent Caprice to do her bidding and wondered if the newcomer sitting in the shadows would accept her offer of being her Prince Charming for the evening. She'd only had to do this on a couple of other occasions and her picks had always been eager, charming and quick learners, yet their cocks had been a little on the small size. For her, size did matter. It just seemed to make the show that much more erotic.

Gosh, she hoped this guy was well-hung.

The rustle of clothing grabbed her attention and Caprice entered the back room where Ella had sequestered herself to mentally prepare for the next scene. It would be her first meeting with the prince.

But who would it be? The sexy newcomer? Or Merck?

"He's agreed."

Yes!

"You've told him everything required of him?"

"He knows what to do. I've got him out back getting into a costume."

Double yes!

"He's quite a hunk. You picked very well, Sin," Caprice complimented as she popped out a compact from nowhere and applied lipstick. "I know he's a lot younger than me, but I think I'm going to have to see if I can't get my hands on him tonight after the performance."

Over my dead body. The thought popped into Ella's head without warning. The intensity of her need to have this stranger all to herself frightened her.

Oh dear. Not good. She couldn't afford to follow these lusty feelings. She needed to keep her mind on the performance, not on the man.

"Sin, ready in five," another performer said as he popped his head inside the room. It was the father of the prince.

She nodded to the man.

Excitement flared as she headed to the door. And to meet her Prince Charming.

Chapter 3

Roarke swallowed against the sudden bout of nervousness as he awaited his cue to enter. He'd been decked out in some unbelievably tight pair of leotard shorts that really enhanced his package.

He'd been stunned when a woman had asked to speak to him privately. She'd whisked him out of the performance room and inquired if he'd mind being Prince Charming to Sinderella.

Hell, he hadn't even thought it over. Had simply reacted and said yes he'd love to. When she'd given him the directions of what would be expected from him during his first scene, it had made his cock hard as stone. So hard he now ached like a son of a bitch. Yet he wasn't really sure he could go through with this. He'd never acted in front of an audience.

Actually that wasn't true. He'd done many gyno procedures

on sedated women in front of a viewing audience of students. This could be similar . . . unfortunately he hadn't been required to take off his clothes, among other things.

Roarke swallowed the tightness in his throat and took a few deep breaths to dispel his nervousness.

Concentrate! Concentrate man!

From the door he peeked into the room to see what was happening.

At the moment Sinderella was being chastised by her stepsisters and stepmother for slacking off on her cleaning duties. The pout on her pretty lips slammed into his stomach like a rocket. Those gorgeous lips reminded him so much of Ella. He shook his head at his craziness.

Not possible. Ella would never have the nerve to do what Sinderella had just done. Masturbating in front of a crowd of onlookers took guts. Ella was too shy. Too sweet and innocent.

Most likely she'd be curled up tonight on her couch with her head in a medical book sipping coffee. He found himself chuckling at that thought. Found himself realizing he wouldn't mind cuddling on a couch with her, kissing her ruby-red lips.

Shit! Why did he keep thinking about Ella when he had this luscious woman right in the next room?

"You're not allowed to peek. Come away from there." It was Caprice, her hand curled around his shoulder, and she was pulling him away from the door.

"Sorry," he muttered. "Just trying to get rid of some of that stage fright."

"Don't worry. Sinderella will be quite pleased with you."

Her interested gaze dropped down to parts south. "She picked well."

"She picked?"

Shit! He sounded like an excited schoolboy.

Caprice nodded. "She seemed quite flustered when she asked me to seek you out."

Really? This was damn good news. He'd thought he'd been selected from the audience at random. Now that he knew Sinderella was just as interested in him as he was in her, it made things a little more interesting and a lot more intense.

"Have you memorized what you're supposed to do?"

Roarke nodded. Oh yes, and he'd be surprising Sinderella with a few tricks of his own. By the time he was finished with her, she'd be begging to know his identity and she'd be very eager to rip off that sexy silver mask of hers so they could get to know each other a hell of a lot better after the show.

Ella swallowed at her suddenly tight throat as the traditional trumpet blew announcing the arrival of the prince. This next scene entailed Sinderella's first meeting with his royal highness . . . the prince had been to far away lands searching for a wife but had come back empty-handed. Now he was on his way home and had run out of water and was very thirsty.

As he entered the room, his face concealed by a sparkling blue mask, Ella's pulses began to pound in wicked anticipation.

God! He was built! He wore nothing but skintight shorts that perfectly outlined his huge cock and swollen balls.

Ella licked her lips. Very nice! Very nice, indeed.

"Hello! My lovely wench," the prince said as he neared her. His deep, masculine voice sent shock waves coursing up her spine.

God! It had to be Roarke!

Hot eyes peered back at her through the slits in the mask. Excitement flared and her body heated with fierce awareness as he read the handful of lines Caprice had given him to remember.

"I'm very thirsty," he said. "May I draw some water from your well?"

Oh dear! If this was Roarke . . .

"I'm sorry, my Prince, but the well is dry."

She could hear his breath quicken, could feel her throat grow dry as he drew closer, as she awaited his next words.

His gaze locked with hers. Although she could barely see his eyes in the darkness of the mask, the sensuality of his look seared into her like a rocket. So intimate she almost forgot about the audience watching them.

"Then you wouldn't mind if I quench my thirst upon your lusty body?"

"I . . . I don't know. I should seek permission from my family, but they are not at home," she replied.

"I'm too thirsty to wait. Would you have my death upon your head?"

"No, I could not. I must submit to you, my Prince."

Readying herself to sit on the chair, she gasped as his hands seared into the naked flesh of her waist. Masculine heat hugged her as he pulled her into a tight embrace.

What the hell? This wasn't part of the performance.

"First a kiss from your sweet lips for a parched man," he said softly.

Oh boy, a kiss was not in the play.

She could feel the coiled tension in his body. The soft press of his chest against her breasts. The rock-hard cock branding her lower belly.

Her cunt quivered, whether out of fear of his massive size or out of excitement, she wasn't sure. He gripped her waist tighter, as if sensing her confusion.

Then his head was lowering and the breath in her lungs stalled.

For a moment she thought of turning her head away. Of regaining some measure of control, but the instant his warm, firm lips touched hers, her body became lost in a swirl of lusty tensions.

She could barely think as his tongue speared into her mouth.

Possession.

Desperation.

Desire.

Eagerness. She sensed it all in his heated kiss.

His mouth burned into hers as he explored. His tongue smoothed over her teeth, mated with her tongue. The brand of his hands slid down her body, cupping her naked ass cheeks. The push of his thick bulge against her lower belly grew harder. The intimate gesture made her vagina clench with primal demand. She found herself melting against his hard contours. Boldly pressing herself into his erection.

He groaned. It was a sensual sound. One like she'd never heard before.

She shivered. Fire raged through her veins. She could barely draw in a breath when he abruptly broke the intoxicating kiss.

She couldn't resist him as he led her to the chair by the fireplace and made her sit. She watched as he got down on one knee between her widespread legs. The wicked burn of his fingers over her knees had her grabbing the edge of the chair just to keep herself steady.

With a quick tug, her thong left her body.

"I'm so thirsty . . . you will not deny me a drink from your well." His voice sounded strangled, aroused.

How could she resist? She couldn't even speak. Couldn't move. Her body felt so tight with anticipation. Her breaths came in such harsh gasps.

"Your pussy is as red as wine," he said, the tip of his tongue peeked out from his luscious mouth. The sight mesmerized her. Sent her pulses careening.

He leaned his head between her legs, his hot breath blazing against her pussy.

"Oh, God," she found herself whispering, her performance lines totally forgotten as she noted his black hair tied back in a ponytail low on his neck.

It had to be Roarke!

She could never have imagined in any of her fantasies, the anticipation, the sweet torture gathering inside her at the sight of Roarke going down on her. Since he was a newcomer without experience in acting, Caprice had instructed him to simply place his mouth over her pussy, allowing her to fake the orgasm. But the strong, moist tongue that licked between her pulsing labia made her just about come out of her chair. She couldn't help but cry out at the fire of his touch and the erotic bristle of his stubble rasping against her tender flesh.

Sweet mercy! Roarke knew how to orally pleasure a woman.

For the first time in her life she allowed herself to simply feel.

And it felt damn good as he sucked a plump labia into his mouth. The heat of his lips branded her. His teeth nibbled gently on her flesh. Fire raged. He seduced her other labia in the same way. Then slid his tongue over and over her clit until her fists turned into tight knots and her lower belly clenched erotically.

When his tongue dove into her slit, she simply came apart. Blades of pleasure zipped through her and she barely heard the strangled cry ripped from her throat as Roarke's tongue plunged in and out of her like a miniature cock. Shudders ran rampant.

Tossing her head back, her lips parted to allow her pants to escape.

His tongue continued the erotic thrust. His nose acted like a clit stimulator, pressing, smoothing, until pleasure spiraled and her cream gushed down her channel.

Slurps quickly followed as he drank greedily from her.

Erotic sensations continued to tear through her, and when he finished, she felt weak from the climax.

"Thank you for quenching my thirst, oh beautiful wench."

Her pussy still fluttered in the glorious aftermath and she found it hard to open her eyes at the sound of his voice.

When she did, he was licking her cum off his lips. His chin and nose shone with her juices.

He remained on one knee and she trembled in awe at the way his chest muscles rippled as he released her legs.

"You taste so sweet, like wine. What is your name, lass?"

The soft caress of his words almost had her telling him her real name. She caught herself at the last moment.

"Sinderella, my Prince."

"Sinder . . . ella." Her name rolled off his tongue in two syllables. The Ella part more pronounced.

Her pulses faltered in a sudden bout of fear. Did he know her true identity? But how could he? She always borrowed a friend's car to come to the performances so no one could trace her. Always removed any jewelry from her body that would give her identity away. Unless he'd recognized her voice? Surely if he had, he would have said something.

No, she was just grasping at straws. He had no idea who she really was.

He stood.

"Alas, my thirst has been quenched as it has never been quenched before. I shall never forget your hospitality or you."

He bowed and then he was gone. Leaving her staring after him. Wanting him. Needing him.

The audience clapped. It was a roar unlike any she'd ever heard before and it sent tingles of happiness slithering up her spine. Obviously they'd enjoyed the performance just as much as she'd enjoyed what Roarke had done to her. The applause faded.

She trembled when she heard the laughter of her approaching stepfamily. It was her cue to continue straight into the next scene. A small scene with her two stepsisters and evil stepmother complaining how tired they were after a day of shopping.

It took every ounce to gather her wits to continue on track with the play. She'd never found it so difficult to concentrate on her lines. Fire laced her cunt. Sticky dampness clung to her inner thighs as she quickly retrieved her thong and tied it back into place.

She wanted to go after Roarke. Wanted to grab him. Push him up against the wall and just fuck him. She blew out a tense breath.

God! She'd never had such a fierce urge to be fucked. To fuck.

She wanted more of those delicious licks he'd given her. At the same time, her mind whirled in disbelief.

Had she really been mouth-fucked by Roarke? Or had she just fantasized it was him and actually given his face to the newcomer?

Passion pounded through her as she suddenly remembered the other delights in store compliments of her Prince Charming.

"Fuck! You lucky dog, Roarke. I've been trying forever to get inside her pussy. How did the bitch taste?" Merck was laughing and slapping congratulations on Roarke's back as Roarke changed into yet another pair of skintight attire. This time he would wear nothing but a thong.

Being practically naked in front of people who knew him made him a bit nervous, but Merck's crude comment about

Sinderella sliced deep into his gut and he resisted the urge to take a swing at the man.

"You'll never know, will you?" Roarke growled.

Merck backed up a step, obviously picking up on his hostility. "Take it easy, man. She's just a slut."

Roarke saw red.

Before he knew what happened, he'd grabbed Merck by his shirt collar and pushed him up against a nearby wall. The sharp sound of a whoosh as the wind left Merck's lungs and the way he blinked back at him—totally stunned—made Roarke regain his senses. However the red-hot anger remained.

"You're a fucking asshole," Roarke hissed, and let go of Merck. "She's not a slut. She's an actress doing her job."

"And it seems her pussy cream has drugged you, my friend." Merck chuckled as he straightened his tie. "Maybe I'll have to get myself a little taste too."

Before he could tell Merck to back off, the bastard had already slipped away.

Clutching his hands into fists, Roarke fought the anger. He was being ridiculous. The woman in the play was just an actress. She was used to having a man's mouth on her pussy. It was part of the act. Caprice had instructed him that because he wasn't trained, he would only have to place his mouth over Sinderella's cunt and she would simply fake the rest. However, when he'd gotten between her legs, he'd been enticed by her overpowering scent of arousal. He'd simply had to taste her, pleasure her, fuck her with his tongue.

Roarke closed his eyes and stifled a moan. She'd tasted so fine. Addictive like a fruity, expensive ice wine. The intense way her vaginal muscles had eagerly clenched around his tongue . . . well, he knew she'd been pleased with the oral sex he'd given to her.

No faking orgasms tonight, Sinderella. Not if he continued to get his way, which by the way her shoulders had tensed up as he'd leaned closer, led him to believe she wasn't used to not being in control.

When he'd pulled her against him, he'd sensed her fear, her indecision.

She'd fit perfectly against him. Soft flesh in all the right places. Her curves melting against his hard planes. She was even the same height as Ella.

Not to mention how innocently she'd kissed. As if she were inexperienced.

Roarke's eyes snapped open at the thought.

Jesus.

Could Sinderella be more innocent than she let on?

"Here's the new dress for the Prince's Ball as promised," Caprice cooed proudly as she entered the back room where Ella had sequestered herself, the harsh, crinkling sound of plastic following her inside. "And before I present it to you, I have to say you did a fabulous performance with the prince. He really brought out the best acting in your career. You really looked like you were climaxing." She wiggled her eyebrows and laid the unwrapped dress on a nearby chair.

"I was climaxing," Ella admitted, still trying to settle her nerves over what had just taken place with Roarke and what would be coming during her next meeting with him.

Caprice's mouth opened in shock. "No way, are you serious?"

Ella nodded.

"Oh, my God! I specifically told him what to do, and going down on you was not in my instructions."

"Obviously he has problems following the rules."

"Obviously. And what was with the kiss? You've never allowed a prince to kiss you before . . . at least not until the last scene."

"I couldn't stop him." Hadn't really wanted to.

"Like hell. You ever hear of slapping his face?" Caprice snapped. "I cannot believe he would take advantage of you like that in front of an audience. I've always told you I do not like it when you pick right from an audience. It's too risky. We should have cancelled tonight's performance. I'm going to have a chat with that man and tell him we've got rules." Caprice started for the door.

"No, don't. I've got my own revenge plans for him."

"Ella. We're professionals. We've got a pristine reputation. We can't afford to screw it with games."

Ella smiled. "Don't worry, Mom," she said using Caprice's nickname affectionately given to her by the troupe. "I'll stay on track with the show. There won't be any surprises." Except for Roarke. A surprise he'll truly enjoy.

"Now get rid of your frown and let's take a look at that sexy new dress you made for me."

"Just remember, my sweet Sinderella, miracles are happening every day. All you have to do is believe in the magic. Believe

in the magic of miracles and a miracle will come true for you," her fairy godmother cooed as she and Ella stood in the middle of Sinderella's living room. Her stepsisters and stepmother had already left for the Prince's Ball, leaving Sinderella crying and desolate that she was prohibited to go because she had her cleaning duties to attend to.

She'd wanted so badly to see the prince again. Wanted so badly to have his mouth on her pussy again.

"But I do believe in the magic of miracles, Fairy Godmother."

Sweet mercy! She really did believe in miracles tonight. Especially now that she'd had the pleasure of kissing the man of her fantasies. Of having his head between her legs, licking and sucking on her cunt, making her experience the best orgasm she'd ever experienced in her life.

"Then close your eyes, Sinderella. Close your eyes and believe in the magic of miracles."

"But I cannot attend wearing these rags, Fairy Godmother."

"Believe it and it will happen."

She closed her eyes and knew the cinematic smoke would gush through the performance room.

"Hurry, hurry," Caprice said. Ella's eyes popped open, and it took only a quick tug on her halter and thong and she stood naked in the smoke. Lifting her arms, she allowed Caprice to slide the slinky dress over her. It fit like a glove.

Personally she'd always wished for a fairy godmother. Someone sweet and nurturing like her motherly friend who would help her garnish her self-esteem and self-confidence. Someone who would grant her wishes and make all her dreams come true, someone who would banish her insecurities around men she felt sexually attracted to . . . men like Roarke.

She'd never had sex with a man without her mask. In a way she was a relationship virgin. Always avoiding men because she didn't really know how to act around them. Didn't possess the self-confidence or self-esteem to be bold enough to go after Roarke, no matter how much she craved to.

She knew she shouldn't, but she'd always blamed her father for her troubles. For him being such a damn fool in picking the wrong woman for himself and for her, thus ruining her childhood. She'd been only five when her beautiful mom had died in childbirth. Her baby sister had died a day after, leaving Ella without a mother or a sibling. Her father became so obsessed with his private hospital that she rarely saw him anymore. At that point her craving for his attention grew and her interest in becoming a gynecologist just as he was took root.

She still remembered the amused way her father had laughed at her when she'd told him in her naïve five-year-old, defiant stance that she wanted to skip school for the rest of her life so she could go to work with him and learn everything about his doctoring trade.

His laughter at her newfound dream had stung. Had ripped a hole in her soul. He'd merely patted her on the head like she was an amusing dog and ushered her off to school with the nanny he'd hired. A year later he'd married a gynecologist who worked at the hospital, saddling Ella with two stepsisters. They were horrid creatures, already in their early teens. They ignored her and studied hard so they could go to medical school and be doctors themselves. They garnered all the attention from her father and new stepmother, leaving her totally alone and frustrated.

In turn, Ella threw herself into her fantasy world. Studying ballet, taking singing lessons and doing anything that would keep her mind occupied at her growing insecurities that she would never be the doctor she wanted to be.

One year later her father died of a massive heart attack, leaving her an unloved stepchild who was shipped off to an all-girls private school so fast it had literally made her head spin. Over the years in the school she'd continued her dance lessons, singing lessons and even taken acting classes.

When she graduated, her stepmother presented her with the trust fund her father had set up with the provision Ella study gynecology and become a doctor so she could carry on with the rest of the *family* in the family business.

In the end, she had succeeded in what she'd wanted to do with her life. She had become a doctor. Unfortunately all her studying and seclusion in her fantasy world hadn't prepared her for interacting with the opposite sex. Hence her creation of Sinderella, which enabled her to hide behind a mask as she dabbled in sex with strange men. Men who seemed to fall in love with the fictional Sinderella, but not really with *her*. Well, maybe if she'd given them the chance they would have loved her, but she'd been unable to remove her mask to get intimate with them.

"And now, sweet, sexy Sinderella, you will go to the ball," her fairy godmother's voice made her snap from her thoughts. "Just remember you must leave the ball before midnight for then the beautiful, sexy clothing will vanish and you will return to the rags you had before."

The audience clapped their appreciation as Sinderella was ushered from the room to await the next scene with her prince.

Roarke blew out a tight breath as he heard the audience clapping and whistling in appreciation.

Shit! They really seemed to be enjoying themselves.

He wished he could be out there in the audience seeing what that sexy woman was up to. But he'd only be squirming impatiently in his chair. Craving her, needing to be inside her, wanting to know exactly what kind of a woman would be bold enough to masturbate in front of a live audience as well as allow a complete stranger to go down on her with thirty or so people watching them.

His cock pulsed violently against his thong and he almost groaned out loud at what would transpire between them at the ball.

"It's time," Caprice said as she and the rest of the troupe, all decked out in sexy, sultry party clothes, moved like one well-oiled machine toward the door.

He was impressed he had to admit as he followed them out into the hallway straining his neck in order to catch a glimpse of his sultry, sexy Sinderella.

To his disappointment she was nowhere to be found. A sliver of frustration nibbled at him. It made him wonder if the real Prince Charming had felt this same kind of frustration when he'd gone about town placing glass slippers on women's feet, hoping to find the woman who had eluded him at the ball.

Oh shit, get this crap out of your brain, man. It's just fantasy.

Short of ripping the mask from her face, he might never find out the woman's true identity. At least that's what he'd learned from the group of actors who, after working with her for a couple of years, still didn't know the identity of their boss. They'd also explained about what had happened to the other princes who'd fallen for the elusive Sinderella. One by one they'd become frustrated with not being able to find out who she was and had quit.

He wouldn't quit that easily.

Before the night was out, he would have her silver mask in his hands or, at the very least, have a way of finding out her true identity. Of that, he was certain. No sane man would put up with what had transpired between the two of them in front of the audience tonight and not want more from her.

Chapter 4

Ella twisted her fingers into anxious knots as she waited outside the door to where the play was taking place. Cripes! She wanted so badly to get a look at her prince. Wanted to push open the door. To run inside and tell him she was Ella. That she wanted him to fall in love with her and *not* with Sinderella.

Caprice seemed to sense her need and kept her figure smack-dab in her way, preventing her from so much as taking a peek through the door at the prince who by then must have danced with Sinderella's two evil sisters. One anorexic. The other extremely overweight.

When Sinderella had been looking to hire the sisters, she'd made sure they reminded her of her own stepsisters. It gave her a morbid satisfaction during the performances when she ended up with the prince and not them. Perhaps this was her immature way of acting out against her own stepfamily.

Whatever the reason, she'd never been so nervous about performing in her life as she was tonight. Come to think of it, ever since she'd caught sight of Roarke's shadowy figure she'd been on the sexual edge of hell.

"I've been told your prince is just as eager to get together again with you as you are with him."

Oh dear. Now she was even more nervous.

Mom smiled softly. "Do you by any chance know him?"

"Good God! Why in the world would you ask that?"

"Because I've never seen you like this before. Your cheeks are so flushed and you're trembling. Not to mention the way you seduced that dildo duster and kept your eyes glued in his direction when you orgasmed—it was as if you were making love to him and not the audience. You should know that's a no-no, Sin. Work the audience. That's always been our number one rule."

"Sorry, I'll do better." God! She couldn't believe she was actually apologizing to her employee.

"Sweetheart, I know you will. I just thought I should mention it."

"I'm glad you did, Mom."

She needed to concentrate. Needed to make this a fantastic performance. Merck was a very rich man and he had deep pockets. The friends he brought here also had deep pockets. They paid handsomely to see the private production.

The sound of a trumpet announcing her arrival snapped her to reality. It was her cue to enter.

For a split second she hesitated.

Dare she go in there? She could screw this up because of her nervousness performing with Roarke.

"Go, go, go," Mom whispered.

Ella nodded and took a deep breath. Renewed gasps of approval zipped through the air as she entered the room dressed in the beautiful, sultry, skintight dress. Of course while she'd been out of sight, there had been a couple of surprises added, but her audience and Roarke would discover it soon enough.

The loudest gasp came from Prince Charming who stood in the corner in front of the king and queen, his parents.

The intense way he watched her made her breath ram right up into her lungs. If looks could undress her, then this man was doing it.

For the first time since she'd started Sinderella, she wanted her mask to be smaller . . . to be gone.

His mask gone.

As she approached Roarke, he simply stood there and stared at her. His intense gaze caressed her skin. Made her feel hot all over.

She wore the sexiest, clingiest, tightest white spandex mid-hip-length dress. The material shimmered with the wet look and hugged her every curve to perfection. The front had an adjustable lace-up cord that revealed her belly button and could reveal as little or as much of her breasts as she wanted.

In anticipation of tonight, she'd left the strings so loose that her prince would have little trouble getting easy access to her.

She shivered beneath his hot stare and the room grew deathly quiet as he moved toward her. His steps were long, confident. It made her heart race with excitement.

His cock seemed so much bigger now. The swollen

outline nestled between two perfectly shaped spheres fired her blood. Velvety muscles laced his chest and a sexy shadow of black stubble caressed his cheeks. This time he wore a sparkling white mask, the color contrasting wonderfully with the thick black hair he now wore loosely over his shoulders.

He was a devastatingly handsome man. A man she wanted in her bed with his hard, long cock plunging in and out of her in uncontrollable thrusts.

At those thoughts she could feel her breath coming faster, harder. Could hear his breath getting louder, raspier, as he held out his hand. Such a wonderfully large hand. A hand meant for caressing her skin, for touching her breasts and a whole bunch of naughty things.

"Shall we dance?" he asked in a low voice that melted over her.

She nodded. Placing her fingers against his warm palm, she immediately sensed the erotic tingles of awareness zip through her. He pulled her close, pressed his body intimately against hers. Pushed that wonderful bulge tightly against her lower abdomen.

Her pussy reacted immediately. Grew hot and wet. Her vaginal muscles clamped around empty air.

She found herself moaning out loud.

Oh, God!

"Have we by chance met before? You seem familiar to me, my Princess," he asked, saying the lines that were expected from him. She sensed he wasn't acting. He was serious.

"Anything is possible, my Prince," she replied.

He smiled and she noticed immediately he wasn't the best of dancers when he stepped on her toes.

Music filtered through the room. They danced to a slow waltz, gazing into each other's eyes as if there weren't thirty people watching them.

And for Ella they were alone.

He moved against her in a sensual rhythm. One hand at her waist, his fingers branding through her clothing. His other hand remained intimately intertwined with her fingers.

His cock burned against her, making her blood pump strong and fast. She found herself answering his rhythm by softly grinding against him, slowly swaying her hips. He inhaled sharply. She noticed his jaw clenched.

Her mind reeled with happiness. He was just as turned-on as she was.

They remained silent as they danced, but she could feel his hot gaze beaming through the mask, burrowing into her skin like a blast from a furnace. When the music finally came to an end, she was breathing so hard and so fast in anticipation of what would come next she actually felt a bit faint.

"Who are you?" He whispered the words so softly she wasn't even sure he'd said them.

Suddenly his head lowered. She trembled and held her breath, thinking he was going to kiss her, instead his warm lips nibbled along the side column of her neck midway between her ear and her shoulder. The erotic touches sent ripples of shivers tingling up her back making her body tighten with exquisite need, and she couldn't stop the soft whimper that escaped her mouth.

He stayed there at her neck, his demanding lips nibbling at her tender flesh. Sucking gently at first, then harder until a sweet burst of pain from his sharp teeth made her whimper again. He calmed the fire he'd created with long, wet strokes of his tongue until her flesh throbbed wonderfully before he pulled slowly away.

Then he spoke, his voice a low, tortured whisper so only the two of them could hear. "I would make love to you right here and now, up against the wall, but I want our first time to be alone."

Her body tightened against his words.

The lights dimmed setting the next scene.

"You're a very beautiful woman. Very desirable," Prince Charming said louder this time so the audience could hear.

"I find you quite irresistible, my Princess."

"And I you," she replied, her heart now beating against her chest like a battering ram.

Oh boy, did she ever want him!

She trembled as he reached for the string holding her corset dress in place. It only took one pull and the strings loosened, allowing him to slide the material over her shoulders, allowing her breasts to spill free in front of him.

And in front of the audience.

She heard the soft inhalations from some of the men. The excited whispers of women when they noticed she wore nipple rings with thumb-sized sparkling glass slippers attached.

Prince Charming was breathing hard. His Adam's apple moved wildly as he swallowed.

"Exquisite breasts," he said hoarsely.

She'd had her nipples pierced a couple of years ago. It allowed her to dress her breasts in some unique ways for her show. By the way Roarke sounded, he certainly appreciated how she'd decorated herself.

He licked his lips and Ella followed the movement of his rosy tongue. Sexual hunger roared through her. She'd never been turned-on so hot and so fast by the sight of a man's tongue.

She held her breath as his head lowered toward her right breast.

She moaned out loud at the whispering impact of his wet tongue teasing the tip of her pierced nipple. Gasped as he placed his lips over her entire pink nipple, including the ring with the dangling glass slipper.

He sucked. Hard.

Lightning streaks seared a line from her breast straight into her pussy.

More! She wanted more!

Automatically her legs parted. Oh boy, did she ever want his mouth down there too.

Her urgency made her moan. Made her want him to rebel against the story line and simply take her pussy with his cock.

Sharp teeth nipped at the tip of her aching bud. Pleasure-pain sliced through her breast. Sensitive nerve endings shimmered as his fingers cupped her other breast, squeezing, kneading, massaging, making her flesh swell with arousal.

At the same time he continued to savage her nipple. His fierce licks, sharp nips and long pulls made her moan louder.

When he had finished tending both her breasts she felt drugged. Drugged with pleasure-pain. It left her so hot and achy she just wanted his cock buried deep inside her. Even with all these people watching.

Then his earlier words whispered at the back of her mind.

I want our first time to be alone.

She didn't think she could wait that long.

When he drew away, she reached out to him. She wanted to touch him. To make sure he was real. Make sure he was actually Roarke and not just wishful thinking or another fantasy.

Her fingers hungrily explored the raspy stubble on his cheeks and chin. The smooth curvature of his moist lips. The strong, corded column of his neck.

Her hands splayed over his velvety chest muscles. When her fingernails scraped the tips of his nipples, she heard him groan in response.

Ella smiled.

Payback is a bitch, Roarke. But a very nice bitch. Now it was her turn to get even.

Ella's hands trailed over his hot, tight abdomen. Hard muscles quivered beneath her fingertips. Quivered with anticipation. With need.

She slipped downward to his waist, to where the white thong held his erection hostage. She pulled the material and it fell away.

She heard herself gasp in surprise. Heard the females in the audience gasp in appreciation. Some of the men swore softly, enviously.

Fierce need consumed her at the juicy sight. Roarke was naked. Powerfully naked.

Nestled amid a spattering of dark, curly hair, surrounded by a couple of perfectly shaped, swollen testicles, his cock looked like stone—hard and curved upward against his abdomen.

Her cunt contracted wickedly. He must be at least ten inches long, maybe even three inches thick.

Prime male. Her fantasy man come to life.

Only better.

"Do I please you, my Princess?"

She nodded, her lines totally forgotten. She couldn't take her gaze from the spectacular sight. Roarke was bigger than she'd ever imagined.

She licked her lips. Felt her naked breasts swell, ache. Her pussy creamed. She could feel the warm stickiness flowing down her inner thighs.

"I take it my Princess is at a loss for words."

The audience chuckled, broke her trance.

"Oh yes, my Prince. Oh yes, your size does please me!"

"I've never felt this way about a woman before."

"And I have never felt this way about a man."

"You have made me so horny, my beauty. Pleasure me, my Princess."

He stroked his straining arousal, and his cock twitched like a live wire.

Ella shuddered with longing. Her body hungered for him. She wanted his huge cock buried deep inside of her.

"I will pleasure you, my Prince. I will show you that I am worthy of your intentions."

He made a move to retrieve one of the flavored condoms kept on a nearby chair for such occasions, but she grabbed his wrist, stopping him.

"No, my Prince."

She heard the soft whispers signal uneasiness through the audience.

Perhaps they thought she would deny the prince, or perhaps they were shocked at her break in protocol. Sinderella always practiced safe oral sex with the prince wearing a condom, but this time . . . this time it was Roarke. This time she would make an exception.

"I want no barriers between us tonight, my Prince," she said loud enough for the audience to hear.

His lips tightened. Was it in arousal? Or in disapproval.

"I will trust you. If you will trust me," she whispered softly so only the two of them could hear.

"I'm clean," he whispered back. "And I trust you."

Warmth spread through her at his words and she smiled. Dropping to her knees in front of him, she eagerly opened her mouth and he guided his swollen cock head toward her face. She wrapped one hand around the pulsing base, his flesh felt like lightning-hot, silk-encased steel against her fingers and palm.

Looking up, she saw the controlled set of his jaws, but he couldn't hide the rapid rise and fall of his naked chest. His hard flesh slid between her lips and her tongue immediately dove against the tiny slit in his bulging head. She tasted the salty pre-cum of his arousal. Swirled her tongue around his impressive flesh, savoring his masculine heat, feeling the pulsing veins straining against his rigid cock.

With her other hand she gripped his firm hip, steadying herself. She could hear his harsh breaths split the air. Felt the carefully restrained thrust of his hips as he moved against her. She began to suck his cock. Her mouth a tight suction as he slid in and out, going deeper with his every delicious thrust. She moved her hand farther up the hard shaft to the point where she could safely take some of his length.

Rubbing her tongue along the sensitive bottom of his cock, she took great pleasure in hearing his groans. The erotic sounds sifted through her, warming her pussy, making her cream over and over.

Taking her time with Roarke, she teased his shaft by gently biting down, allowing her teeth to scrape along his tender flesh as he plunged in and out of her mouth.

His groans grew louder, wilder.

His hands speared through her wig, holding her head captive. His fingers tightened against her scalp and she knew he was dangerously close to losing control.

She backed off, relishing his moans of protest.

Oh yes, she had Roarke right where she wanted him—at her mercy.

Her tongue cradled his cock, welcomed him in. But her teeth, ah yes . . . her teeth were just about bringing him to his knees. His cock jerked and pulsed in what she perceived as him experiencing pleasure-pain.

Once again she increased the pressure of her teeth against the frantic plunges. Enjoyed the untamed groans.

She loved the feel of his cock sliding in and out of her mouth. The velvety skin. The rock-hard flesh. The powerful taste of man and musk.

She sucked harder. He thrust his hips harder.

"I'm coming," he suddenly gasped.

In the past, the prince would spew into his condom and then throw it into the nearby flickering fireplace. With the change in protocol, Roarke probably felt unsure of what to do.

Digging fingers harder into his hip, she pulled him closer.

If that didn't give him an indication of what she wanted, she then tightened her lips around his shaft and she sucked with all her might.

"Oh, God!" he ground out as his thrusts came quicker. His cock grew tense. Jerked.

And then she savored what she'd worked so hard to get. Loved the thick jets of his warm semen as he came inside her mouth.

Ella swallowed every drop.

When he was spent, he slumped onto the nearby chair. Crystal beads of perspiration dampened his chest. His eyes were scrunched tightly. His lips parted from his harsh gasps.

Ella smiled despite the arousal roaring through her.

Sitting down wasn't a part of the show, but in this case he'd be excused.

"Did I please you, my Prince?" Her voice shook and his eyes blinked open. A knowing grin flittered across his delicious mouth.

"I have fallen in love with you, my Princess."

"And I with you, my Prince."

The clang of the clock striking midnight made Ella groan her frustration.

Oh, God! Not now. The sound was her cue to run from the ball.

"I must leave," she said, and she stood.

"But you've only just gotten here, my love."

My love. That wasn't part of the script.

In the background the strike of the midnight bell continued to clang.

Oh damn! She didn't want to leave. She wanted to stay there with Roarke. Enjoy more of this fantasy play.

Unfortunately if she didn't go at the strike of midnight, it would ruin the show. She had an audience watching them. An audience she'd totally forgotten in her haste to have Roarke's delicious cock.

Ella headed for the door. Her legs felt weak, her pussy sopping wet and, to her horror, she almost forgot to drop the nipple ring with the glass slipper onto the floor.

"What in the world happened out there? Are you insane? We always practice safe sex! I can't believe what you've done!" Caprice hissed as she and a couple of the troupe ushered her to the nearby dressing room.

"Slight deviation from the plan," she answered truthfully. But she wanted more of the deviation. She could feel the sticky wetness of her arousal wetting her inner legs. Could feel her engorged clit throbbing in desire, her pussy aching to be fulfilled.

A roar of applause, whistles and shouts followed.

"That's the scene ending. He must have found the nipple ring. Why did you do the oral sex without a condom? God, please tell me you had a good reason, sweetheart. Please tell me you haven't lost your mind?"

"Mom, rest assured I do know what I am doing. Please trust me," Ella reassured the frantic woman.

"Okay, okay. I trust you. I do. I really do. I know you do things for a reason."

"Did the audience seem to be okay with it?" She'd been so greedy in not thinking about their reaction. Most of them were from the medical profession. Doctors, nurses and others she'd seen at medical conferences. They would not be pleased.

"I hadn't realized. I was too busy watching the two of you."

Shoot!

"Okay. Spread it around that we know each other. That we trust each other." Her admission of the truth was her only source of damage control. Her only way to show she had been a responsible adult tonight. She truly did trust Roarke. Instincts told her he would never put her in any kind of danger, sexual or otherwise.

"I knew it! You two have a sexual energy that permeates the room. You looked absolutely smashing together and you act so naturally with each other," Caprice cooed. "You obviously enjoyed him. We should hire him."

"No. He can't be my prince."

"Surely we can—"

"I said no!" Ella found herself snapping as reality reared its ugly head. She couldn't chance Roarke finding out about her secret life. He could not know she was Sinderella. If he found out, then her life would be too distracting at work. Hell, with her frequent fantasies about him, it was already too distracting at work. Surely with tonight's experience popping into her mind whenever she saw him, her klutziness around him was bound to worsen.

Oh, God! What was she going to do?

She caught Caprice frowning at her.

"I'm sorry for snapping at you, Caprice. I didn't mean to."

"Well, you're the boss, sweetie," her fairy godmother said calmly, embracing Ella in a hug she really needed. "You've never steered us wrong before. If you don't want him for your Prince Charming, I'll tell the rest of the troupe before they get too excited. I'll drop word to the audience you are intimately involved and trust each other."

"Okay," Ella nodded.

Caprice let her go and smiled warmly, knowingly. "Are you sure you don't want him?"

"I'm sure." Liar!

"Okay, get yourself ready for the next scene."

With a soft rustle of clothing, Caprice left the dressing room.

But I want him to be my prince. I want him to be mine, Ella thought. *All mine.*

Closing her eyes, she concentrated really hard and whispered to herself, "I believe in the magic of miracles. I truly believe. Roarke will someday become my Prince Charming in every way."

Roarke was still savoring the sweet, erotic way Sinderella's tight little mouth had wrapped so perfectly around his penis when a sharp rap at the door cued him to get his ass in gear for the final scene.

He'd never seen a more erotic sight than having this gorgeous woman drop down on her knees in front of him. He'd been told what would transpire. Had been told to ejaculate into a condom and throw it into the fireplace, but when he'd tried to follow the rules, Sinderella had turned the tables on him.

No condom. Her grip had tightened. The sensual way her mouth had worked his cock made him her prisoner. At her mercy.

He'd never known a woman to go down on him so eagerly. So unconditionally. Sweet, sexy Sinderella. The woman of his dreams. His woman in every way.

Or she would be . . . when the time was right.

Chapter 5

I have found you. I have found the love of my life." Ella held her breath as nude from the waist up, Roarke's warm, slightly trembling fingers brushed against her naked breast as he quickly inserted the missing nipple ring with the sparkling glass slipper.

"We will be together. Forever," he said softly, and she accepted the prince's warm hand. His fingers clasped intimately with hers and he squeezed gently when they both bowed, indicating the performance was completed.

The applause was deafening. The audience stood and Sinderella held her breath at the sight.

A standing ovation.

Oh my gosh! She felt so exhilarated. So unbelievably happy.

When Roarke raised her arm and pointed at her, the audience went wild.

Have mercy! They really liked her. She felt herself gush like a schoolgirl.

In return, she raised Roarke's arm. The audience went equally wild.

Oh dear.

As was tradition her troupe surrounded the prince and princess and ushered them safely from the performance room.

A warm blanket was thrown around Sinderella's shoulders and Caprice quickly ushered her into another room away from the troupe.

"Merck wants to see you," Caprice said. Worry etched her voice. "And he sounds serious. Before you tell him where to take his disgusting offer, make sure he pays you first."

Ella had confided in Caprice about Merck's sexual insinuations and Caprice had been chilly with the man ever since, insisting they never perform there again. But Ella had insisted they continue to accept Merck and his generosity for as long as they could.

"I'll handle him, don't worry," Ella reassured her friend as Caprice helped her into a gorgeous red velvet dress that made Ella look both professional and sexy at the same time.

"Sweetie, I always worry about you. You're just like one of my daughters to me and I don't like it when a dirty old man makes unclean advances toward you. So please promise me you'll be very careful with him tonight. I didn't like the smile he had on his face or the way his fingers were groping inside his pants while he watched you and that stranger performing."

"That's why we're here, Caprice. To make our audience horny."

Ella winked as she slipped on a pair of red high heels and headed for the door.

Caprice grabbed Ella by the elbow stopping her short.

"Sin, you're not taking me seriously."

Geez, she'd never seen her friend act this way before.

"Okay, I promise. I will be careful. Really." She patted the woman's hand and Caprice reluctantly let go of her.

"Thanks for worrying about me," Ella soothed. "I'll make sure I get the money before I kick his ass."

"Maybe I should come with you?"

Caprice's frostiness toward Merck wouldn't help the situation. "No you stay here and wait with the crew. I'll be back soon."

Even though she'd reassured Caprice she'd be fine, uneasiness swooped around Ella as she walked down the deserted hallway to his personal office where she usually collected the cash from Merck.

The wooden oak door stood wide open and she readjusted her mask before knocking and entering. She found Merck dressed in a dark gray smoking jacket and matching pants, standing at the far side of the rectangle-shaped room looking out the night-darkened window and puffing on a stinky cigar.

Overhead a crystal chandelier sparkled splashes of bright light against the sultry red walls, tanned leather sofa and the giant, sleek mahogany office desk.

"Ah, beautiful Sinderella. Please come in. Come in." The gray-haired man of seventy smiled and waved her in.

"I hope you were pleased with tonight's performance," Ella said as she took a few steps inside, trying hard to appear confident and strong despite the bulge pressing at the older man's pants when he strolled toward her.

"Please, have a seat. I'll pour you a drink. How about a sherry? I've just had it imported from Jerez in Spain especially for you."

"I'd be pleased to have a glass, Merck." But she'd rather stand.

Despite her uneasiness, she came farther into the room. It was tradition that they share a drink before talking business. Asking for the money due her performers was always the worst part of being boss. But the members of her crew depended on her to get what was rightfully theirs and, until now, she'd never failed them.

Ella watched as he poured the drinks, scrutinizing his every move to make sure he didn't slip any type of date-rape drug into her drink. Call her paranoid, but in her line of business, she knew it was better to be paranoid than sorry.

"Sinderella, I must say your show was exceptionally well done tonight." He handed her the drink in an exquisitely long-stemmed wineglass. She waited until he took a few sips.

"I'm glad to hear you and the audience enjoyed yourselves. We aim to please."

She took a taste of the fruity drink and sweetness exploded against her taste buds.

"Exquisite sherry, Merck. You have exceptional taste."

Merck grinned. Instincts and experience told her it wasn't a genuine smile and tendrils of fear curled through her confidence.

She'd learned in their relationship that flattery got more help from Merck.

"How did you enjoy the new Prince Charming?" The question caught her totally off guard. "I was sure you'd pick me, Sinderella."

He'd moved closer. Way too close for comfort.

"I . . ." How did she tell a seventy-year-old man that she didn't pick him because she just wasn't impressed with him? And if she wasn't impressed, then the audience wouldn't be either.

"I apologize if someone gave you the idea you would be picked, Merck."

Blue cigar smoke twirled from his cigar and stung her eyes. She resisted the urge to move away from him, opting not to show him how uncomfortable she was getting. "But I'm the one who makes the final decisions."

He pouted. "I volunteered long before my friend Roarke did."

Oh for Pete's sake! He sounded as if he were a spoiled child.

"I've decided I want to be your Prince Charming tonight, Sinderella." He reached for her arm, but she managed to step away just in time.

"I'm sorry, Merck. But the performance for tonight is over. I am here to collect our payment."

"And what if I told you I'm not paying until you allow me to fuck you."

"I'd say you'd be insulting the group of Sinderella and we'd have to withhold any further performances until payment is rendered," she said firmly.

Gosh, why couldn't she be this bold with her stepmother and stepsisters? Because she was hiding behind the mask, that's why. Life was always easier when she pretended to be someone else.

His lips twisted with apparent contempt. "Well, then. How's about a little kiss. Your performance with Roarke has gotten me so horny. You let him kiss you. I want to kiss you too."

"Kisses are out of the question, Merck. As I said—"

She cried out in surprise as Merck suddenly lunged and grabbed her by the arm, yanking her against his body. For an old guy he sure was strong!

"What the hell is the matter with you?" She tried to jerk away, but his grip tightened. His eyes seemed glazed and not at all normal. It looked as if he were in some kind of a trance.

She swallowed frantically at the panic climbing into her throat and shivered in revulsion as he rubbed his engorged erection against her thigh.

"I knew you'd like that cock, teasing, little slut," he growled. She grimaced at his acrid cigar smelling breath.

"Let go of me!"

God! She couldn't believe this was happening. Couldn't believe how paralyzed she suddenly felt. She should be kicking him, struggling, but she could barely breathe.

"Merck, please. I'm tired. Just—"

"Oh but, no, I've just begun," he snarled.

Suddenly he pushed her. Hard. Ella gasped as she found herself sailing so easily backward, landing on the couch with a soft bounce. Before she could react, he'd dropped on top of her, pinning her beneath him, his heavy weight knocking the breath clear out of her lungs.

Oh, my God! She couldn't even scream for help, let alone gasp for air. Terror unlike anything she'd ever experienced swooped around her.

"Oh, sweet Sinderella. I want to put my cock into your tight pussy. I want to fuck your brains out."

Get off me! Her mind screamed. She could barely breathe. The bastard felt like a cement block on top of her. His erection burned into her lower belly and she felt totally helpless as she lay trapped beneath him. He'd even trapped her arms or she would have been scratching frantically at his eyes, his face, anything to get him off of her.

"A kiss. Just as you gave Roarke. And then I want to suck on those big nipples and your juicy pussy just like Roarke did. Nice and sweet, I bet."

Her eyes widened with disgust.

"Oh yeah, Roarke was bragging when I talked to him in the dressing room. He told me how I should taste your sweet lips and how the cream from your cunt drugged him. How good he felt with your mouth wrapped around his cock. How he wanted the both of us to get to know you better after the performance."

No way! There was no way Roarke would ever say something like that!

Merck's face drew closer.

"You'd like that wouldn't you, Sinderella? Having two Prince Charmings fucking you?"

His obscene breath seeped into her lungs.

Oh, God! Please someone help me!

She could feel his grubby hand trailing up her inner thigh. Nausea rippled through her belly.

"Let me see how wet you are for Prince Charming, sweet Sinderella. It'll be over fast. You've made me so horny. I'll just stick my cock into your cunt."

"Get the fuck off her, Merck, or I will kill you!"

Merck's body stiffened at the sound of Roarke's harsh voice and Ella said a silent *thank you* for her prince coming to her rescue.

"Oh, my God!" Caprice whispered, her voice laced with the same horror Ella was experiencing.

When the man didn't move fast enough off her, she watched in stunned admiration as Roarke's long fingers gripped Merck's shoulders and he literally picked the man up and stood him on his feet.

"Pay the women what you owe them and leave her the fuck alone!"

"Hey, come on. It's not like she's your girlfriend." Merck laughed uneasily as he brushed at his clothing.

The muscles in Roarke's jaws twitched angrily but he said nothing. He merely stared at Merck in disgust.

"Fine." Merck's hand slipped into a side pocket of his smoking jacket and pulled out a sizeable envelope. "It's all there."

"It better be." Roarke snapped the envelope away. "Now get out of my face before I do something you'll be sorry about . . . if you're lucky to wake up."

"Fuck you, Roarke," Merck grumbled, and then stomped off.

"Sweetie, are you all right?" Caprice was suddenly sitting

on the sofa beside her, enveloping Ella in her embrace. "Thank God, Roarke came with me. I told you Merck was up to no good."

"I'm okay, really," Ella whispered, quite thankful for Caprice's strong arms holding her tight.

"Caprice," Roarke said gently. "I think you'd better get the money to the troupe and tell them to leave. There won't be any more performances here."

Caprice nodded and pulled away. Her friend looked totally defiant and ready to fight if Ella didn't agree. "He's right. We can't come here again. Not after what's happened."

"Please don't tell the others," Ella whispered, feeling shame heat her cheeks as Roarke frowned at her in the background. She avoided his gaze. Did he think because of the way she dressed and the way she acted in Sinderella that he had the right to gossip to Merck?

Oh damn! Now she really didn't want him to find out her true identity. He'd think she was a whore.

"You've done nothing wrong," Caprice reassured, and smiled warmly. "You have nothing to be ashamed of."

But she did feel ashamed. A man had literally thrown himself all over her without her heeding the warning signs. She'd been stupid to come in there alone.

"Let's please just forget this happened, okay?" She tried to smile at both of them, but her lips just kind of wobbled.

"Okay. I'll go give everyone their share," she whispered, and let Ella go from her embrace.

"Thank you. I'll stay here for a few moments."

Caprice nodded. She looked at Roarke, and then nodded as if to say to herself Ella would be safe with him.

"Are you sure you're all right?" Roarke asked after Caprice left the room. The softness with which he spoke brought tears to Ella's eyes and she suddenly realized the full impact of what had almost happened. She could have been raped by Merck!

"I . . . I'm fine," she said as he sat down on the couch beside her, a severe frown on his face. His body warmth wrapped snugly around her, making her feel just a little bit safe and secure.

"You're shivering."

"Just adrenaline. I'm sure it'll go away in a few minutes. I do have to say thank you," she found herself saying. "I know what you must be thinking. How it looked. I mean I've never seen him act quite that way. He's insinuated things and I've told him I'm not interested, but I never thought . . ."

"No man should force himself on a woman. If there hadn't been witnesses, he'd be dead now."

Ella blinked at the fierceness in his words.

"I'm sorry. He must be drunk . . . I didn't mean to break up your friendship—"

"Christ, woman! He's no friend. And don't make excuses for him! Do you always accept blame for other people's stupidity?" He inhaled and shoved a hand through his luscious-looking black hair.

Oh boy, he was really pissed off. Even when he was mad he looked sexy.

"I'm sorry. I shouldn't have yelled at you. He's a disgrace to mankind. I'm glad I've seen his true colors. Although, I'd rather it have been under different circumstances."

"Spoken like a true gentleman." She found herself smiling.

"Or a true prince. Which leads me to why I was looking for you."

His green eyes glittered fiercely as he held out his hand. She spied the nipple ring with the pretty glass slipper nestled in the palm of his hand.

"You dropped it again after the performance. I thought you'd be needing it."

"Thank you." When she picked it up, her fingertips blazed as she touched his flesh.

"Would you like me to see you to your car?"

"No, I'm fine."

He nodded and an uneasy silence stretched between them.

"I should go now," she said. Yes, she should leave before she told him something she shouldn't. Despite her need to go, she couldn't move. "I guess I should personally thank you for agreeing to be my Prince Charming tonight."

Back off, Ella. Dangerous territory. Get out now while you still have a chance, her mind warned.

Her breath halted in her lungs as he suddenly reached up and caressed the bite he'd given her earlier. His intimate touch created sparkles of warmth. In all the excitement she'd forgotten about the mark. Realized she'd have to find a way to cover it up tomorrow at work so he wouldn't see it.

"I apologize if I went too far. I just couldn't resist you."

Ella swallowed. "I . . . I've never had better," she admitted truthfully.

"I know you're upset about Merck. Maybe I should take you back to my place until you've calmed down."

Oh, God, how she'd love to go back to his place.

"No, I'm sorry. I'm sort of interested in someone." *You idiot! Tell him you're interested in him! Tell him he's everything you've ever dreamed of. Everything you've ever fantasized about. Only better.*

"Sort of interested? Meaning?"

"He's engaged."

"But he's not married. Maybe you would still have a chance with him if you told him your true feelings? I am assuming he doesn't know?"

"No," she admitted, wondering how in the world they'd gotten onto this subject.

"You should tell him. He may feel the same way about you. Maybe he's very attracted to you. You're a beautiful woman."

Oh my gosh. Roarke thinks I'm beautiful? Or does he think Sinderella is beautiful?

"Without the mask, I'm different," she admitted.

"With or without the mask, you're still attractive. You still taste the same. Talk the same. Act the same. Sexy. Beautiful."

Warmth scuttled over her cheeks.

"You're blushing."

"I'm sorry."

"No, don't be. It's very sexy."

Blushing is sexy? Her breathing went shallow.

His intense gaze held her captive. "Does this guy you're interested in know that you do this Sinderella show?"

"I've never told him."

"Why not?"

God! Was he persistent or what?

"Because he might not understand?"

"Hmm. How do you know unless you tell him?"

"It's too big of a chance to take. If I tell him, then he'll know what I do. If he doesn't understand . . ." If he didn't understand, he'd laugh at her. He'd think of her as being a big fool. She'd be devastated. For Roarke not to know might be easier for both of them.

His hand came up and a thumb caressed one corner of her mouth, making her heart pick up speed and her insides quiver with need.

"Is he the jealous type?"

She'd never really thought about that. Was Roarke the jealous type? Would he consider her a slut for having oral sex with strange men? All her fantasies had been about him loving her. Sinderella hadn't been in the picture. Maybe because she had been fantasizing and not really considering reality. That's why she'd never seriously thought about it.

"I don't know if he is," she answered truthfully.

"Why not tell me why you sing and dance and perform in such a luscious story? Then I could tell you from a man's perspective if he might have a problem with it."

Here was her chance to find out exactly what Roarke would think about her. It was an opportunity she might never have again.

"There is one main reason why I perform."

In answer he quirked an eyebrow. The sight made her belly flutter. He looked so sexy when he did that.

"Being?"

She didn't know why she hesitated. But she did. It wasn't

as if she had anything to lose. She actually felt quite comfortable speaking to Roarke with her face hidden. It seemed as if he were suddenly a good friend, a confidant. Hell! He really had no idea he was talking to his klutzy coworker.

"I feel free when I perform," she admitted. "During my formative years I put all my time into working toward a career. It left me with no social skills with men and so now I hide behind my mask." There she'd said it. She'd bared her heart for him and it hadn't even hurt.

"I see." Was that disappointment in his voice? "I'd say the whole thing lies on the premise if this man you're interested in is a jealous type or not. If he is the jealous type, then he would have a very hard time with it, especially if he knew other men were sexually satisfying you and he was at home waiting in the wings so to speak. That wouldn't go over too well."

Shit! How could she find out if Roarke was the jealous type? She could come straight out and ask him. Couldn't she?

"If he's not the jealous type," he continued, "then your relationship probably wouldn't work out. It means he doesn't care enough or love you enough."

"Oh." Now she was more confused than ever.

"But if the man were me . . ."

Ella's breath halted in her lungs as she anxiously awaited his answer.

"But he isn't me so you wouldn't need my opinion on the matter."

Her hopes deflated.

"You said you had a main reason. That means you have other reasons?"

"Well, actually, yes. A very important reason. The money I make I donate anonymously to some local charities for young girls and women."

His eyes widened for a split second and he looked as if he might be surprised at her answer, but then he smiled easily.

"I'd say that's a noble and understandable cause that your man would certainly understand."

Suddenly Caprice's voice echoed down the hall. She was coming back to see how Ella was doing.

"I really have to go."

"So you wish to remain a mystery to me?"

God! Of course, she didn't want to remain a mystery to him. Especially after what he'd just said about understanding why she wished to keep her identity a secret.

But she had no choice. She didn't want to break his engagement. Whatever gave her the idea that she could? She'd seen his fiancée's picture. She was beautiful. Voluptuous. A looker. And his fiancée didn't have the Sinderella skeleton in her closet like Ella did.

"Ella, come on, honey. I'll walk you to the car." Caprice stood in the doorway.

Before he could say anything else, she headed for the door. She half expected him to follow as she left with Caprice.

He didn't.

Disappointment rocked her, and by the time her friend had her safely tucked inside the car and waved goodbye to her, Ella allowed the tears to burst free.

God! She'd really made a mess of her life, hadn't she?

Tonight she'd had oral sex with the man of her fantasies,

had almost gotten raped by that bastard Merck and now she was letting her Prince Charming go. She was simply no good for his career. That is if he truly had wanted her and not Sinderella as he'd said.

Roarke listened to the grandfather clock in the hallway ring the twelve bells.

Midnight.

For real this time.

Frustration grabbed at him. Instincts told him he should follow her home and confront her.

Fuck! Why had he allowed her to go so easily? Be-cause Merck's house wasn't the place to tell her how much he wanted her.

He'd wait. But not for long.

He turned to leave when a shimmer on the floor caught his eye.

Sinderella's nipple ring with the glass slipper. She must have dropped it again on her way out.

Roarke frowned and picked up the delicate item.

Now he understood how Prince Charming must have felt when the real Cinderella had left the Prince's ball.

Shitty. Real fucking shitty.

Chapter 6

When she'd first come to work at Cinder her stepfamily had stuck her in an office in the doldrums of the hospital. They thought she'd be intimidated at being told there hadn't been any more office space in the mainstream area of the hospital her father had created. Instead, they'd accommodated her with a spot in the basement. In an empty room.

She hadn't been put off. Not in the least.

She craved solitude and her cozy office allowed her the quiet she needed to do her paperwork quickly and efficiently. Of course, the way she'd decorated it had helped. She'd done it in one weekend. Had painted the back brick wall in a soft yellow and done the rest of her office in a cheerful wallpaper that made it look like an artist had dumped red, green and yellow paint everywhere.

Of course, her stepmother had been horrified, but Ella had forced herself to take a stand. Had refused to submit to having a painter come in and drown her artistic endeavor with puke green paint as everyone else's office had been decorated in.

As if she could call a bile green color as being decorative. She'd further mutinied by purchasing a gorgeous desk with steel legs topped with a thick sheet of clear glass. It housed her bright red designer computer. She'd also lugged into the colorful mix her comfy yet tattered ergonomic computer chair. Sleek white miniblinds hung on the wired glass window of her office door, ensuring her privacy.

Lining the wide hallway just outside her door, she kept her huge floor-to-ceiling filing cabinet with her patients' files.

Speaking of patients, she'd just been given China Smith's lab results and was in the process of scrutinizing it when Roarke's soft voice zipped through the air making her breath still in her chest.

"Why don't you turn that frown upside down?"

Her head snapped up and she watched, transfixed by those gorgeously wide shoulders, as he strolled into her office and stopped in front of her glass desk.

The muscles in her lower belly clenched wickedly as his masculine scent swept around her, capturing her, making her tremble with fierce need.

"I just looked in on China. She's doing exceptionally well. She can be released soon," he said.

It was late in the day and he had that sexy stubble of beard growing. God! It made him look so much like a bad boy!

Ella cleared her suddenly dry throat.

"I know. I've just been looking at her latest test results. She and the baby are going to make it."

"And the reason for your frown is?"

"She's homeless unless she returns to her pimp, which she is considering. I'm racking my brains trying to get her some help. If I can get her deemed as an adult and get her welfare, she can find an apartment—"

"There are other options."

"If you're talking about sending her back to her family, that's totally out of the question. She ran away in the first place because her stepfather was sexually abusing her."

Now it was Roarke's turn to frown. "We can get her into foster care."

"Won't happen. I already mentioned it, and she doesn't trust adults."

"She trusted you . . ."

"Only because she heard about me through a good friend, or she wouldn't have come here. She trusts no one in any type of authority. Her stepfather is a cop . . . she's afraid if she does trust any adult in authority, the same thing will happen to her again."

"And being a prostitute is different?" he snapped. His eyes blazed with a sudden burst of anger that rattled Ella.

"Her pimp is fifteen," she explained.

Roarke swore softly.

She wasn't normally a person who pried into other people's business, but the look of anguish flaring across Roarke's face made her bold.

"Sounds to me like China's story has hit a nerve. You care to tell me about it?"

"You want to tell me why you're wearing a silk scarf around your neck?"

She froze at his question.

"The scarf makes you look quite sexy," he continued. "But personally, I prefer to see your neck bare."

She found herself searching his green eyes. The hurt was still there, but it sparkled amid other emotions.

Lust. Desire. Sexual need.

"Do you always use changing the subject as a self-defense mechanism?" she whispered, suddenly understanding Roarke the man. He wasn't as complicated as she'd thought. There was another side to him just as she'd suspected.

"You're a quick study, aren't you?" he grumbled, but she noted the sweet pull of amusement tipping his lips.

"Only when you show me your tender side," she admitted. She found herself answering his smile and felt her old glasses move down the bridge of her nose as they always seemed to do lately. Quickly she pressed the metal frame against the bridge of her nose and caught him watching her. Suddenly she could barely breathe.

"You look really sexy when you do that, Ella."

"I do?"

His comment totally caught her off guard.

"Very sexy."

Oh dear.

He smiled. "I can get China into a home for unwed mothers. I have pull there. I run it."

"Oh? You run it?"

He didn't strike her as the type of a man who'd actually do something like that. Obviously she had a lot to learn about him.

"You sound surprised that I actually have a heart."

His eyes appeared to have darkened as he looked at her.

"Um . . ." Gosh she didn't know what to say.

He turned and headed back for the door again. For a moment she thought she'd offended him by not saying anything and now he was leaving, but he didn't go.

He stared at the closed door for a moment and said softly, "You really should get a lock for the door."

Her heart thundered at the sound of his thick voice. He turned around and she instantly recognized *that* look. The searing look that made her face flame.

He wanted her.

As he came toward her, she felt nervous. Boy, did she feel nervous!

His big size made the room seem awfully small.

"Wouldn't want us to get interrupted."

Her eyes widened at his statement.

Sweet shit! He wouldn't try anything in her office, would he? Her pussy tightened at that thought.

"I guess I should tell you the truth about why I accepted this position at Cinder."

Ella blinked in confusion. One minute he acted sexy as sin, the next minute he was in confession mode.

"I know your father left you as a co-owner, but I don't feel disloyal telling you that I took this job strictly for the money and I don't really give two shits about the rich snobs who Cinder targets."

"You don't?"

"No, and I'm pretty sure you don't either."

He slipped his lab coat off and let it fall to the floor. He began to unbutton his shirt.

Oh my goodness!

"I need the money for a home I help run with my mother. The state only gives us a certain amount and we have a tendency of using it up before the end of the allocated period. The government doesn't seem to realize how much prenatal care girls really need when they are pregnant. So I took this job to help finance my dream."

"Which is?"

He shrugged out of his shirt. She couldn't seem to keep her eyes off his naked chest. Couldn't forget the feel of the hard bunch of chest muscles she'd touched last night.

"A soft place for teenage mothers to fall is our dream. A soft place my mother didn't have forty years ago when she was at the age of fourteen raped by a neighbor. Scandal forced her onto the streets."

"You were a product of rape?"

"No, my brother was. When she was on the streets, a pimp got his clutches into her. He forced her to give him up after he was born. She's never been able to find him. He brainwashed her, stole her self-esteem and used her for almost five years before she ran off with a john of hers. They got married and I'm one of two kids they had. My mom was one of the lucky ones."

Ella swallowed. "I'm so sorry about what happened to her when she was young."

"Don't be."

His fingers were now unbuttoning the stud at the waist of his jeans.

Oh dear!

"My mother always says bad things happen for a reason. You just have to search for the positive side and use it to your advantage. If things hadn't happened the way they did, then my mother wouldn't have told me her stories and I wouldn't have this passion to help unwed mothers. My girls wouldn't have A Soft Place To Fall."

"That's the charity—" She cut herself off. She'd been about to tell him that's one of the charities she donated her Sinderella money to.

The sound of his zipper made her return her attention to his waist. His jeans were now open, riding low on his hips, exposing a tight pair of black underwear and a delicious arrow of crisp, black curls.

Ella blew out a tense breath.

"But don't let those she-devil stepsisters or stepmother know, they just might have a heart attack that their colleague might actually have a life outside of Cinder, unlike themselves."

He stood very close to her now.

"I'm good at keeping secrets," she found herself whispering.

"I know you are."

His hand was at her neck, untying the knot on her scarf. Before she could even simulate thoughts in her mind to find some form of protest, her neck was bare.

Roarke's eyes blazed. "Just as I suspected. Sinderella, I

presume." He stroked a lone finger along her sore hickey, the brand he'd left on her neck last night.

His breathing seemed rough now. Uneven.

Her heart pounded. Roarke knew her secret!

"How did you know? When did you start to suspect?"

"You had me the instant I first heard you singing. Deep down, somewhere inside me, I knew it was you, but I just couldn't believe sensuous Sinderella was the same as sexy-assin Ella, the woman I've been craving to fuck since the first day I saw you."

Ella's cheeks flushed with heat.

"What about your fiancée?"

"Actually she's my younger sister who lives overseas. We had pictures done the last time she came for a visit. I used one of them."

Holy! He was unattached. There was nothing keeping her from pursuing him. The idea seemed overwhelming. Almost too good to be true.

"You didn't name any names last night when you mentioned the charities you donate to, but I'm assuming you are the anonymous donor for A Soft Place To Fall."

"I am," she confessed.

"My girls appreciate your help. We'd be hurting without your generosity, Ella."

His fierce gaze never left her face as his finger moved lazily up her flushed check to caress her chin. She trembled at his soft touch.

"I can think of one hell of a good way to thank you for donating to our cause."

"I don't expect any thanks. I do it because I enjoy giving."

"And I enjoy receiving."

Sparks of hunger speared through her as he leaned down and his lips slid hungrily against hers. She couldn't even think to hesitate when he yanked her to her feet beside him.

His mouth remained erotically fused with hers, his tongue dueled with hers.

Hunger gnawed deep inside her empty cunt. His hard body pressed against hers, firing her arousal.

He broke the kiss. His eyes blazed as his fingers quickly opened her blouse. Her breasts were swelling against her bra. Cool air washed over her suddenly bare shoulders as he pulled the blouse off. His hot fingers curled beneath the elastic of her pants, his touch searing her skin, making her cry out at its intensity. With a quick, desperate tug, he had her pants down around her ankles. Then her thong underwear joined them.

He jerked both of them and her shoes off her feet.

She cried out as he lifted her and slammed her bare ass upon her cool, glass table. Reaching around her, he unclasped her bra and whipped it aside. They were both breathing roughly, the sounds shooting through her office like bullets. She could feel the slick juices escape her vagina, probably smearing her tabletop.

He spread her legs wide. Stepped between them. The sight of his heavily muscled chest just about made her come on the spot. His eyes were wild. So wild.

She watched as he slipped his jeans and underwear down over his hips releasing his cock.

Thick and long, the huge bald head flushed an angry purple. Her nipples hardened at the sight, her pussy creamed more.

"You're so fucking beautiful, Ella." His voice sounded strangled, heavy. His eyes glittered with lust. "I want you so fucking bad. I can't wait any longer. I've held myself back for so long. Pretending not to care just because I didn't want to mix business with pleasure. Too many months of fantasizing."

She fought for breath at his admission. He'd wanted her just as badly as she wanted him?

Oh yes! There was a God!

"I want to bind you. Whip you. Fuck you a hundred different ways. I want you to be my fantasy girl, Ella. Every day, every night."

Ella couldn't stop herself from moaning as she remembered her own fantasy scenes with the same themes.

"Last night when I saw Merck touching you against your will, I wanted to kill him. I don't want another man near you. I am the jealous type. I care too much about you to let another day go by without showing you how I've felt about you all this time. I want to be your man and your Prince Charming in your future Sinderella productions."

Her pussy spasmed as he stroked the long length of his cock. Her body heated with longing.

"You haven't officially been interviewed for the position of my Prince Charming," she teased.

"Then we'll do an interview now. You can let me know later if I passed. Lie back on the desk."

His unexpected order made her blink in confusion. This was happening way too fast. She could barely get her mind around the fact that she sat naked on her office desk in front of Roarke without her mask and his fierce, hungry gaze was zeroed in right between her legs.

"Trust me, sweet Sin."

She loved his nickname for her and did as he asked, lying backward on the table, the smooth, cool glass caressing her ass and back.

She yelped as his hot hands sidled around her ankles and he hoisted her legs up, spreading them as he placed them over his rock-hard shoulders.

"Play with your breasts," he ordered.

As he watched her, she did as he said. Her heart pounded out of control as she looked down at her two mounds and touched her sensitive nipples. She didn't wear her nipple rings today because her nipples were still so sensitive from Roarke's attentions last night.

The instant she pinched the tips, pleasure flared.

"Keep playing with yourself," he demanded.

She did. She watched her breasts swell and her nipples turn hard and rosy beneath his fierce stare and her intimate touches. She cried out as an unexpected finger smoothed over her clit, unleashing the carnal cravings lusting inside her. It took him only seconds and he had her on fire, her pussy soaked and aching to be filled, and her breaths reduced to cries.

With a growl he thrust inside her.

Deep. Hard. Intense.

Ella exploded. *Oh God! This feels too fucking good to be real!*

Erotic pleasure tore through her as Roarke's thick,

powerful cock plunged in and out of her, making her breasts bounce wildly beneath her hands. Suctioning sounds split the air. The scent of her sex filled her nostrils.

"Oh yes! Roarke, fuck me! Fuck me harder!" she gasped, and kept pinching and tugging her sore nipples, tossing her head to and fro, thoroughly enjoying the carnal spasms making her tremble.

Suddenly from the corner of her eye she detected movement. Realized the office door had opened. Someone was standing there! Her stepmother! And her two evil stepsisters!

"Oh, God!" she cried out, stunned at the increasing arousal screaming through her at knowing the bitches were watching Roarke fuck her.

Another climax gripped her. Lust, raw and carnal roared through her. She closed her eyes and drowned in the pleasure that Roarke's wickedly delicious cock gave so freely. His finger continued to massage her ultrasensitive clit and he just kept pumping into her.

Hard and fierce just as she'd asked. Oh yes! Beautiful!

"Get the fuck out of here!" she heard Roarke growl at them. But he didn't miss a beat as he continued to pleasure her.

"This is shocking behavior!" her stepmother stuttered.

"What Ella and I do in the privacy of her own office is none of your fucking business. Get the fuck out! Now! And knock next time."

The slamming of the door barely registered as Roarke continued with his deliciously hard thrusts. Her pussy continued to spasm. Her body lost in a storm of pleasure.

"First thing we do is get a lock on that door," he ground

out. His hips pumped faster, his cock roared in and out, driving Ella to more carnal sensations.

"I want you to be the woman of my fantasies, Ella, and I want to be the man in yours."

"You already are my fantasy man," she admitted.

He grinned that incredible sexy grin she loved, and when she started coming down from her third fantastic orgasmic high, she felt Roarke's hot jets of sperm filling her.

Epilogue

Several weeks later . . .

At the sound of the door to the examination room opening and closing softly, Ella bit down on the ball gag in her mouth with wicked anticipation.

Oh God! Roarke was here!

Roarke, who'd turned out to be a more fierce lover than even her wildest fantasy. After the day her stepmother and stepsisters had caught Roarke making love to her in her office, Ella had gloated at their envious looks.

He'd invited her to move in with him and they'd been practically and literally inseparable ever since. From that time on, she'd also learned that having people watching her have sex was only one of her many sexual fetishes. She enjoyed being whipped, craved being taken by Roarke compliments of the doggie style and loved having her nipples clamped.

By day they continued to work at Cinder Hospital catering to the rich and snobby, yet slowly implementing new rules using her part ownership in the hospital to loosen restrictions so Ella could care for low-income and homeless pregnant girls and women who needed them the most.

Some evenings she helped Roarke and his charming mother at A Soft Place To Fall. His father worked there also. He was a tall, older version of Roarke, extremely jovial and fun to be around. His mother was sweet and so affectionate that she felt safe and loved by the older woman who Ella believed would have been an ideal mother for herself.

A few nights a month she also continued being Sinderella with a disguised Roarke as her Prince Charming. Despite Merck not being involved any longer, the carnal act had expanded quickly based on word-of-mouth alone. They always closed to a standing ovation.

When Roarke got her alone, he continued to surprise her with a variety of delightful pleasures such as tonight when he'd brought her to one of the examination rooms at the hospital that contained a rigged-up gyno table where he'd instructed her in what to do to ready herself for him.

"All ready for your examination, Ella?" His deep voice ripped her back to the present and her pussy spasmed with excitement. She swallowed at the rustle of clothing being removed and blew out a shaky breath through her nose at the sound of his bare feet padding closer to her.

Her cheeks warmed as he suddenly stood beside the gyno table where he'd instructed her to strap her feet into the cool, silver stirrups and to lash restraints over and under her breasts securing her.

She inhaled a quivering breath as Roarke's hand smoothed over her wrist, bringing it to her side. The snap of Velcro quickly followed and she automatically pulled against her bond. Nothing budged. He did the same with her other wrist, binding her. Making her his captive. Putting her at his total mercy.

Oh boy.

"You okay?"

Ella nodded. Bondage was something she'd always wanted to try. Now she had the chance.

I trust you, her mind whispered. Her body tingled at the warmth flooding through her. She was lusciously naked and ready for Roarke's intimate exam.

"Let's start with your breasts."

She couldn't help but whimper around the gag as he looked at her full mounds. Her nipples responded immediately to his hungry gaze, blushing a beautiful burgundy color as they hardened into knots.

"Very nice. I can see your breasts are in great condition."

Did she detect huskiness in his otherwise confident voice? For a moment he left her view, and when he came back he held a small whip in his hand.

Oh sweet mercy!

Her pussy contracted. Creamed in anticipation.

"You ready?"

She nodded. Braced herself.

The whishing sound of the whip sailed through the air. Pain snapped into her left nipple. She jerked in reaction.

Watched her tip turn red with anger. Her tummy clenched. Her pussy grew warm.

Pulsed.

More lashes. This time on her breasts. Blistering heat mixed with pain. She bucked against her restraints with every lash.

Bright red stripes interlaced her globes. By the time he finished with her breasts they burned and her pussy was creaming up a storm.

"Are you horny, Ella?" His strangled question made her avert from his lusty gaze. Heat fused her face. Her body tightened with exquisite need.

"No answer? Hmm, I guess I'll have to examine your pussy."

Ella's thighs tightened with need as Roarke moved to the foot of the table. Her legs were spread wide. Her feet held captive by stirrups and her heart pumped madly at the anticipation in his green eyes when he noticed the wide base of the butt plug in her ass.

"Very nice, Ella," he complimented.

She bit against the ball gag as his hands glided softly along her inner thighs toward her pussy and her plugged anus.

A single finger smoothed over her clit, bringing instant pleasure.

"You're so fucking responsive, Ella," he groaned. She knew he loved the way she reacted so quickly to his touch. Knew it meant she craved him just as much as he yearned for her.

His finger dipped into her vagina, smoothing back and

forth, massaging her G-spot until she shivered and whimpered beneath his sensual touches.

The pleasure built swiftly and she twisted against her restraints.

Please! Fuck me! Her mind screamed. God! She loved Roarke so much. Loved the things he did to her body, the sexy way he made her feel.

"Let's get rid of that butt plug so I can fuck your tight little ass, shall we?"

She nodded eagerly, her mind screaming at him to hurry. She'd always wanted to experience anal penetration, but hadn't had the nerve to ask. When he'd broached the subject several weeks ago, she readily agreed. She'd worn the various sizes of plugs. Allowing them to stretch her, to fill her, prepare her for him.

The last one, the huge one was just about as big as his cock and now lay buried inside her rear end.

"Before I fuck your tight little ass, I've got a present for you."

Her eyes widened as he produced a large, black glass wand. It looked to be about ten glorious inches long with a straight shaft at least two inches wide with one half-inch smooth swirls and dots webbed along the entire length. And the stylized, round glass head looked so wonderfully huge.

"I had it made just for you, sweet Sin. I call it the pleasure rod."

Heat spread through her as he dipped the glass wand between her legs. While he massaged her clit with the round head, she groaned at the pleasure the rod created.

A moment later she felt the sex toy pushing into her. Stretching her. Making her moan as the smooth ridges and dots caressed her insides.

He began to thrust it in and out of her. She arched her hips, silently demanding more pleasure. Wanting harder thrusts.

"You are insatiable, Ella. I love that about you. I love everything about you," Roarke groaned.

And then the glass wand stopped, and through her sexual haze, she heard the slurpy sounds of Roarke dipping his fingers into the jar of lubricant she'd noticed earlier on the nearby table when she'd first entered the exam room. She whimpered her excitement as he liberally applied the lube to his cock. Smearing every glorious inch of his thick, pulsing, rigid piece of flesh.

She found herself flushing as he leaned forward, felt the butt plug move. Strange sensations she rather liked gripped her anus as he slowly pulled the object from her body.

His breathing had quickened. Her heart raced with anticipation. She groaned around the ball gag as a generously lubed finger thrust inside her ass, pressing past her now loosened sphincter muscle. Despite his finger feeling so small compared to the huge plug, incredible sensations wrapped around her as he moved in an erotically slow exploration. He groaned. "I can't wait to fuck your sweet little ass."

The glass wand was on the move again, slipping across her engorged clit with a delightfully hard rub.

Sweet pleasure flared in her pussy.

"Your virgin ass isn't going to be that way for much longer, Sexy Sin."

Roarke slipped another generously lubed finger into her anus making her moan at the foreign intrusion of two hot, slippery fingers widening her. Invading her.

He slipped the glass wand into her tight cunt. The large ball stretching her. Filling her soaked pussy.

In no time flat he had her moaning at a gentle yet insistent rhythm of both her channels being gloriously filled. Her thighs clenched tightly. Her body hummed.

Oh wow! It felt unbelievable.

"I can tell by your wide eyes, you are pleased."

Pleased was an understatement! She bit down on the ball gag as a third lubed finger thrust into her tender ass.

Oh God! His fingers were stretching her ass so incredibly full. The glass wand slurped in and out of her snug cunt making Ella moan beneath the dual thrusts.

Perspiration dotted her skin. Her harsh breaths came fast and tortured.

"And now, Sweet Sin, brace yourself."

She whimpered as he withdrew his fingers with a slurp and guided his angry-looking, stiff cock closer to her splayed-out body. When the hot, lubricated cock head pushed against her sphincter, she couldn't help but cry against the gag in wonder at the odd sensation.

Keeping the glass rod impaled inside her soaked cunt, he pushed his long, thick cock into her ass. Immediately his face became an image of tortured pleasure. And he'd barely penetrated her.

"Oh yes, Ella. Your ass is so tight."

He pushed into her ass farther. She felt her eyes widen in wonder at the sudden burst of pleasure-pain.

He'd warned her about it. Warned her to simply keep herself relaxed and breathe into it. And that's exactly what she did. She focused on the pleasure-pain while he kept his hungry gaze glued to her face, to her eyes, watching her carefully.

She knew he searched for her safe signal of three rapid eye blinks for him to stop if she felt she couldn't endure it. But she didn't want him to stop. The exquisite intermingling of pleasure mixed with sweet pain had her craving for more.

His thick cock filled her ass—her muscles eagerly gripped his hard, hot length. Her thighs clenched as his hard cock burrowed deeper.

Sweet mercy but he was long! She could feel every hard, delicious inch of his rigid flesh buried deep inside her.

He kept the wand on the move. His thrusts becoming quicker, fiercer. The smooth glass ridges seared into her vagina, making her forget exactly how big an intruder his cock felt as he impaled her ass.

Without warning he pulled his cock out and speared back into her again. She whimpered at the brilliant onslaught. The dual thrusts became faster. Erotic sensations flared. Her body tightened, flared with wicked pleasure.

She closed her eyes and breathed into the glowing eroticism as it exploded all around her.

Sweet carnal sensations.

She convulsed beneath his hard thrusts. Exquisite spasms tore through her. She could barely assimilate what was happening.

"Beautiful, Sin! Just fucking beautiful!" Roarke's pleased voice ground out so far away.

As he came inside her, she simply allowed herself to float into the erotic bliss all the while her mind kept repeating over and over again, *Oh yes, Fairy Godmother, I believe.*

I believe in the magic of miracles because my miracle came true.

Wolf in Cheap Clothing

CHARLENE TEGLIA

Chapter 1

blonde walks into a bar . . .

Louise Catrell figured it was her way of coping with anxiety when the opening of a bad joke was all she could think about as she stood just outside The Big Kahuna. But it was going to be fine. No need to get nervous. She would blend right in with the crowd of surfers and college students who frequented this beachside Southern Californian bar.

Surfer music poured out into the night and mixed with the sounds of the wind, the waves lapping at the shore and the drone of traffic on the nearby highway, all so normal that it soothed her nerves.

She glanced down at her clothes. The bikini in a bright watermelon shade that barely covered her nipples and covered even less of her ass was more than some of the women who'd gone in ahead of her wore. But even in her attempt to play Beach Slut Barbie, Lou couldn't quite bring herself to parade around like that in a risky situation. So she'd added a denim miniskirt. It bore more of a resemblance to a really wide belt that hugged her hips than a skirt, but between it and the bikini bottoms, she felt slightly more protected. Although the effect of her C-cup curves mostly exposed struck Lou as borderline pornographic. It was almost more suggestive of a harness than a bikini top.

The white canvas sneakers instead of sandals were a calculated risk. She didn't want to have to kick off her shoes if she needed speed, and they suited the casual but sexy look she'd cultivated. A denim jacket hung over her arm since the outfit didn't leave her any place to store her wallet and car keys. She wanted to wear it and add another layer of protection, but she was there to attract attention, not hide from it.

Her bleached-blond hair was pulled into a bouncy ponytail and contrasted nicely with her heavy black mascara and hot-rod red lipstick. With any luck her appearance would do all the work for her. Picking up a guy would be as easy as fishing with dynamite. Really, it was almost cheating.

You look like a cheap slut, Lou, she encouraged herself silently. *Perfect. Now embrace your inner bimbo and go get him.*

Right. With a deep breath that threatened what little modesty her bikini top retained, Lou straightened her shoulders, tilted her chin up and went in.

As soon as she opened the door, the full volume of the music hit her. She was practically going to have to shout to be heard. Another good reason to let her clothes and her body do as much of the talking as possible.

Fortunately, her body had plenty to say on the topic she

wanted to broadcast. There was a swing in her hips and an ease in her stride, an earthy sensuality in her movements that came from being a very physical creature at home in her skin. Even her scanty outfit didn't disturb her aside from the scanty protection it offered. Smooth bare skin was so easily damaged.

A year ago she hadn't been like this at all—relaxed and sensual and physically alert at the same time. She'd been a tense, hurried woman in a business suit, uncomfortable with herself and her world. Always trying to perform, to project the right tone. She hadn't enjoyed the sheer physical pleasure of being alive, feeling the sun or the wind on her skin, savoring flavors on her tongue. Well, she was very aware of the pleasures of being alive now. Nearly getting herself killed had done all kinds of things to her perspective.

Lou worked her way over to the crowded bar, angling herself sideways when she had to, sliding through dancers and people talking in groups. Once she reached the wide oak bar, it was easy to catch the bartender's eye. A quick glance told her the rest of the crowd was drinking beer and Jell-O shots. Ugh. Well, she had a cast-iron stomach. With a mental shrug, Lou indicated with a nod of her head that she'd have what everybody else was having.

Her Jell-O shot and draft beer appeared in front of her with impressive speed. This bartender was really earning his tips tonight. Either that, or she'd won him over just by standing there jiggling.

She jiggled a little more than she had to while she dug out her wallet and pulled out a bill. He deserved it for being such a nice boy.

A male hand covered hers just as she was sliding the money over the bar. "Let me buy you a drink."

It wasn't a question. He was making it a statement. Pushy. Lou knew without even looking that he wasn't the one. Still, she turned her head to see what kind of fish she'd hooked.

He was big and good-looking for now, but his habits would start showing in his face and his body within a few years and then he'd lose what little appeal he had. He wouldn't know that, however. He was sure he was God's gift to women. His kind wouldn't go away without a push, and she couldn't have him hanging around getting in the way.

A subtle push, though. She was supposed to be an easy lay, not the type to rip a man to shreds.

She let a little of her true self show in her eyes and leaned close, letting her nose nearly touch his before she answered. "You're looking for somebody else. I turn into a real bitch once a month and it's almost that time."

Nobody else who was standing nearby would see or hear anything amiss. She was smiling and keeping her body loose and relaxed. From any angle she would look anything but threatening. All the threat was in her eyes and her voice, pitched so only Mr. Wrong could hear.

He didn't take it well but he backed off. "Stupid bitch," was the best parting shot he could come up with. Lou barely kept herself from shaking her head. Really, he was so far out of his league it was pitiful.

Not like the one she'd come hunting for. That one was a predator and he would take all of her skill to handle. She'd done her best to prepare. She had the advantage of surprise.

She'd stacked the odds as far in her favor as she could manage. But she didn't kid herself that it was going to be easy with him.

And then suddenly he was there. She felt him, her skin prickling with the sense that she was being watched by something dangerous, long before she saw him.

He was dressed to blend in like she was and it was just as certainly a costume. Silk Hawaiian print shirt worn open to expose a broad expanse of chest and washboard abs tanned a nice shade of golden. Denim jeans with the top button undone. Scuffed leather deck shoes over bare feet. Dark brown hair worn long enough to show the natural curl and streaked with gold from the sun. Little lines around the corners of his brown eyes that made it look like he was smiling when he wasn't. Everything about him said California beach lover, except for the eyes. They were too sharp and watchful to match the lazy, good-times pose.

Lou looked around the bar and observed the rest of the crowd with her senses on full alert, comparing and cataloging. She didn't think she was mistaken. He was the one, the wolf in the crowd of harmless sheep.

And he was going to come right to her.

She made eye contact with him and lifted her Jell-O shot in an almost salute. She tipped her head back slightly in a move that lifted her breasts and bared her neck as she put the glass to her lips and let the contents slide down her throat.

He was beside her before she settled the empty glass back down onto the bar.

"Hello."

She liked his voice instantly and wished she didn't. It had a deep, husky timbre that made her want to growl in response.

"Hello, yourself," Lou answered. Her voice was as Midwestern as his and that was the clincher. He didn't belong here either. He wasn't any more of a local than she was, but he'd been here long enough to acquire the tan. That fit. The one she'd come looking for had vanished from Michigan almost a year ago and all signs pointed to this California bar as his new hunting ground.

Up this close she could see that his eyes were more amber than brown, flecked with gold. Wolf's eyes. He smiled at her and she wanted to smile back. Since it was in character, she let herself.

"Can I buy you a real drink?"

What an opening. She took it. "Now that you mention it, I have a real craving for Sex on the Beach." She put enough jiggle in bending toward him to make a lesser man's eyes cross and enough innuendo in her voice to make her meaning clear to a man with the density of plutonium.

"Really." His smile broadened. "I think we can work something out. Do you want to finish your beer first?"

"Absolutely." There wasn't enough alcohol in either glass to endanger her. It would take a whole lot more than a couple of drinks to overpower her new metabolism, but it might take the edge off her nerves. She chugged the beer without hesitation and slid the empty glass next to the shot glass. The bartender had picked up her ten-dollar bill and placed her change on the bar already. She left it for him.

Then she curled her hand over her wolf's arm and felt the

surge of something powerful and surprising spread through her from the point of contact. It took a real effort of will not to tighten her hold on him, not to lean into him and slide more of her bare skin against his to heighten the effect.

She hadn't felt anything like that before, but then, she'd changed. Lou forced herself to focus on the task at hand and let him lead her out into the warm, waiting night while The Beach Boys sang an incongruous accompaniment.

Nothing really bad ever happened in the endless summer world of The Beach Boys. Whatever happened tonight, Lou was pretty sure it was going to be bad.

When he slipped behind her and snapped handcuffs on her with inhuman speed, it confirmed the bad feeling.

Chapter 2

This is so sudden." Lou pitched her voice seductively low to cover the waver of alarm in it. She wiggled the hands currently cuffed behind her back and went on, "Usually there's some small talk and foreplay before the handcuffs come out."

"Nothing stopping us from talking now," a lazy masculine drawl pointed out from behind her. Very close behind her. "And as for the foreplay, with handcuffs on you it means I have to do all the work."

Dammit. He was seriously going to leave her like this. Lou closed her eyes and cursed inwardly. Out loud would feel better, but it would also ruin her current persona of party girl on the prowl.

The evening was not going according to plan.

"Look. This is a little fast for me." She shifted forward,

away from his body heat and his breath on her bare shoulders. "I don't usually do bondage on the first date."

"We're not dating," he pointed out. "We're not even having a one-night stand. You picked me up in there and brought me outside to have sex on the beach."

"That could take all night, if you do it right," Lou said, starting to feel annoyed. Honestly. Men. "We didn't exactly get specific in the bar. It was too noisy. I didn't say I wanted you for a five-minute quickie."

"You implied you could be easily satisfied." A hand trailed down her spine, toyed with the silky fabric of her bikini top and then slipped inside the waistband of her almost a skirt.

A hand that belonged to a total stranger. A stranger who might be a killer. And she was helpless. Shit, shit, shit.

"Seriously, you have to let me go for a minute. I need to get something from my car." Lou leaned back against him, letting her body relax into his. Strangely easy to do, given the circumstances. Something about him made her want to rub against him and luxuriate in the contact.

"And then you won't object to me putting the cuffs right back on you?"

"Hey, if it means you'll do all the work . . . " She let her voice trail off into what hopefully sounded like a sexy laugh and not hyperventilating panic.

"And what's in your car that's so important?"

A *gun. Loaded.* "Condoms, silly."

"I have condoms."

Just her luck, he was prepared. Or was he lying to her? "Let me see," Lou demanded. She tossed her head, a movement that made her blond ponytail tickle his bare chest. Hopefully it distracted him.

She felt his body shift, felt his hand slide into the front jeans pocket that her barely covered butt was now plastered up against and heard the crinkle of a foil-wrapped package. He reached around her bare waist to display it on his open palm. "There."

"It's too dark," she hedged. "I can't see what kind. I always use ribbed and lubricated."

"Picky." His voice was clearly amused. Well, that was something. It beat homicidal rage. "I'm in charge of foreplay, remember? Lubrication won't be a problem."

"What about the ribs?" Lou decided it was perfectly in character to harp on that point. A real party girl would demand ribbed for her pleasure.

"I think you'll find me adequate without enhancement." The hand holding the condom pressed against her belly, molding her butt more firmly against the hard ridge of his erection. Lou felt her eyes widen in surprise. Adequate? That was an understatement.

She dragged her mind away from his demonstrably adequate equipment and back to the sticking point. He wasn't going to be talked into letting her go. Which might be fine if he really didn't have anything but uncomplicated sex in mind, but there was that *if*.

"I know what you're doing."

Cold fear knifed through her belly. "W-what do you mean?"

"You're stalling." His other hand came around her waist,

slid low and rubbed a slow circle over her mound, subtly stimulating her clit. The thin denim fabric of her skirt felt like an incredibly inadequate layer of protection between her flesh and his hand. "Are you afraid to submit to me and ask for my protection?"

"That's it," Lou said, latching on to his explanation. Then she realized it made no sense at all. "I mean, what?"

"You're a strange female in my territory." His breath touched her bare neck seconds before his lips did. "You're unmated. I'm the alpha. You have the right to ask for my protection and the protection of my pack if you submit to me."

"Um, I think you have the wrong girl." She shivered. His lips had no business feeling seductive and wonderful on the curve of her neck. But then a lot of serial killers were probably practiced seducers, which was how they got their victims alone and vulnerable.

Teeth closed over her neck and bit into the skin. "Ouch! Look, this has gone far enough. I've changed my mind."

He let out a low growl. It resonated over her skin and slipped underneath, making something inside her hum in response.

To Lou's disbelief, her body betrayed her. Her head fell back, exposing her throat to him. He was alpha and she was submitting to him.

Terror filled her. This was it, the nightmare she'd lived with for so many months. Teeth were going to slash and rend her exposed flesh, her blood would spill, her bones would shatter. She'd survived before, but what if he recognized her and made sure to finish the job this time?

"You taste like fear." There was a new sound in his voice. Rough, aroused, animal.

"No shit," Lou sobbed out. If she'd been able to move, she would be fighting for her life, but some insane paralysis held her captive.

"Has the alpha of your own pack hurt you, little wolf? Is that why you're afraid?"

There was something besides arousal in his voice. Anger. It fueled her panic and suddenly Lou found she could overcome the instinct to submit with the instinct for survival. In a fury of motion she used her feet, the weight of her body, the metal of the handcuffs, everything at her disposal fueled by inhuman strength and agility to fight for her freedom.

A human male would never have been able to hold her, handcuffed or not. But this was no human male. This was an alpha werewolf in his prime, and not even the extra-strength terror lent her was enough to break free.

He subdued her. He forced her to the ground, facedown, and pinned her there with the full weight of his body. She fought on, trying to break his hold, until finally all her strength was gone and nothing but defeat remained.

Lou went still underneath him then, vibrating with a mixture of fear and fury at the inadequacy of her body. Her new senses, her new strength, none of it was enough.

"I guess that's my answer." He picked up the conversation easily, as if she hadn't just done her best to maim him for life. "You're not going back to him."

No, of course she wasn't. She wasn't going anywhere, ever again. This was it.

Lou closed her eyes and waited for her life to flash in front of her. It didn't happen, which was probably just as well. The last significant event in her life was being mauled and left for dead and she really didn't want to relive it in her memories just before reliving it in the flesh.

She'd survived only because her blood contained the antigen that triggered the transformation when it mingled with the blood of the were who'd attacked her. Now that she was a were herself instead of a human female, he'd be more thorough. There'd be no miracle to save her this time.

She huddled into the sand, still warm from the sun, and waited for him to strike.

"Still with me?" His lips grazed along her neck and nipped lightly at her earlobe. "I'd feel bad about this right now, but you picked me up. If you like it rough, I'm okay with that. Rough play can be fun. But that didn't feel much like foreplay to me."

Oh, hell, he was going to get chatty first. Why didn't he just kill her and get it over with? She couldn't stand it, she really couldn't. "Don't drag it out, for heaven's sake. Just do it."

"And you wonder why I got the impression you didn't want a man who could go all night." Amusement tinged his voice. "You'd probably bitch at me later about insufficient lubrication if I just did it. Wrestling in the sand with me just now didn't get you wet?"

"Like it matters," Lou growled.

"It matters. I have a reputation to think about. And I know your type. If I don't make sure you come at least three times, you'll go back inside and tell everybody I'm lousy and probably a premature ejaculator. The men won't respect me. All the women will spread the word. And I'll never get laid in this town again."

He sounded aggrieved. He was laughing at her, the jerk.

"Didn't your mother teach you not to play with your food?" she snapped back.

That made him laugh outright. "Is that your subtle way of asking if the big, bad wolf is going to eat you?" He tugged at her ponytail and nuzzled her earlobe. "If you wanted oral with your bondage, you only had to ask."

Lou let out a strangled shriek of frustration. She was going to die and he had to pick now to play comedian.

He hadn't been nearly this good-humored in Detroit. Lou frowned and thought about that. Which was difficult, with him nuzzling and nibbling at her, toying with her barely dressed body and generally creating a world-class distraction. But she had a very practical, logical mind from years of working in health insurance claims and she forced it to sort out the facts.

It was a fact that a werewolf had nearly killed her in that alley outside a bar with a reputation for being the local meat market. She'd been passing by, heard a woman scream and run to help. Only instead of fighting off a thug like she'd expected, she'd found the woman being attacked by what looked like an enormous wolf. While Lou watched, horrified, the wolf finished the woman off and she'd quit screaming forever. And then it had licked its bloody muzzle and launched itself at her.

After that she wasn't herself once a month and the lunar cycle took on a whole new importance in her life. She'd been attacked by a werewolf, and now she was one too.

The string of killings around the Detroit bar ended that night. Up until then, five women who'd reportedly been in the bar at some point on the evening of a full moon wound up dead. Most of them had been killed in their own cars, parked nearby.

Then a similar series of murders had happened every full moon in the vicinity of this bar for the last three months.

So the wolf she was after had to be around here somewhere. She'd gone into the bar looking for him, hoping to draw his attention by playing to his type, a harmless-looking girl in search of a good time with an available man. And unless she'd missed something, the only werewolf in the place besides herself was now massaging her hips and kissing his way along her bare shoulders. And making jokes.

There was also the fact that the animal inside her liked him with an enthusiasm never before displayed toward any other person. She'd learned that her animal self had instincts and an inner wisdom that were more reliable than human reasoning, as well as far more acute senses. Now that she thought about it, she didn't really believe her inner wolf was wrong to trust him.

It didn't add up. But he'd called himself the local alpha and mentioned his pack, like he was in charge around here.

Lou's eyes went wide. And he'd singled her out and snapped cuffs on her. Not a coincidence. If she hadn't given him an excuse to get her alone, he would have come up with one. She'd done his job for him. No wonder he was in such a good mood.

He was after the killer himself, and he probably thought he had his man. Woman. Wolf. Whatever.

"That really isn't necessary," Lou said, trying to wiggle away from his busy hands and mouth, although her heart wasn't really in it. And when he interspersed kisses with little love bites, she shuddered in response. It felt far too good. The animal side of herself wanted to get closer, wanted that strange buzz of power that spread from him to her to continue and grow.

"I think we already established that it is. Lubrication, your orgasms, my reputation?" He caught the edge of her skirt and tugged it down her legs. "Although I'm more than happy to just get right to the oral sex if you're ready for me to move on."

"Stop for a second. We need to talk."

"You know, conversations that start out with *we need to talk* never end well. Why don't you hold that thought until after you've had an orgasm or two?"

Lou's teeth ground together so hard he had to be able to hear them. "Now."

He tugged her bikini bottoms down, following the trail her skirt had blazed. "Don't worry, I won't let any sand get into sensitive places."

Since he had her hips lifted up, she was startled to notice, she wasn't in any immediate danger. And then he shrugged his shirt off and slid it underneath her as a protective barrier against grit before stroking his hands along her ass cheeks and pressing them down. "You have an amazing ass."

She closed her eyes and tried very hard not to notice what he was doing to her ass with those busy hands and lips of his, but since it felt pretty amazing, she had to give that up as hopeless. Lubrication was not going to be a problem.

She could feel her sex swelling in anticipation of getting the same attention from him, growing embarrassingly wet in the process. He bit the curve of one ass cheek just hard enough to sting, licked the sting away and massaged his fingers in circles that went lower and lower until they nearly grazed her waiting cleft.

"Talk. Now," she choked out before she lost her powers of speech completely.

"All right, if you insist." He rolled her onto her side and spooned up behind her. And slid one hand between her legs from behind to cup her naked mound, sliding an expert finger around and over her clit. His palm pressed against her puffed-up cunt with a pressure that was both a welcome relief and an even more tantalizing tease. His other arm curled around her from the side. His free hand slipped inside her bikini top to roll a nipple between two fingers. "I think we need to work on the lubrication some more."

A choking sound escaped her. Oh, hell, maybe he was right. Talk was cheap, but a curl-your-toes, roll-your-eyes-back orgasm was priceless. The strange, sizzling something that spread from every point of contact with him and surged through her told her any orgasm she had with him would be a world-class mind-bender.

She wanted that orgasm. In fact, she needed it. Bad. They could straighten out the misunderstanding later.

Urging him on with her hips, Lou slipped one leg up over his to give him better access. He obligingly speared her aching pussy with one finger and then slid another one inside to keep the first company. She made a strangled sound of encouragement and when he moved his other hand down to stroke her clit, she gave up on everything but riding his hands until the promised orgasm ripped through her and drenched his fingers.

It did, in fact, curl her toes and make her eyes roll back, and when the last ripple ended, he continued to use his front hand to toy with her clit and her nipples in turns while his fingers moved inside her from behind until she found herself feeling pretty interested in having another one at his hands. So to speak.

"You have a point," he said, stroking his fingers along her slick and swollen cunt with thorough attention. "There is something I have to say before this goes any further and if I don't say it before I take my jeans off, it'll be too late because my cock is going straight inside you."

Lou's vaginal walls contracted sharply around the fingers still buried inside her at his graphic words.

"I take it you don't have a problem with that."

She should, she remembered that vaguely, but it really didn't seem important now. Especially with her muscles half relaxed from pleasure and half tensed to experience more. What seemed important was getting his wonderful cock inside her, deep inside, riding her hard and fast from behind. As good as his hands felt, she needed more. Deeper penetration. The sensation of having her needy cunt stretched and filled to capacity with his cock. And having him do it to her while she was handcuffed and helpless filled her with heat that outmatched her earlier fear.

"Fuck me," she said in response.

"Do you understand what's happening?" As he asked the question, he slid his hands free of her to strip away his jeans and Lou nearly cried out at the loss. She writhed back against him to keep some part of her in contact with him, needing the touch of his flesh against hers even more now.

"Yes. Apparently getting handcuffed by a stranger turns me on. Hurry. Get naked," she snarled back. She'd never felt this before, this fire, this building feeling inside as if some strange power had been summoned by his touch and it needed to keep building until it was big enough to do . . . something. She had no idea what, but she knew instinctively that they had to keep touching, that they'd started something that couldn't be stopped without concluding however it was meant to.

He rolled her up onto her knees and nudged them wide apart. She could feel the head of his cock, hard and ready, right where she wanted it. His hands slid under her and supported her hips since with her hands cuffed uselessly behind her she might have collapsed flat to the sand with his first thrust.

Lou waited for it, the strange, coiled thing inside her waited for it, until the sense of building power nearly choked her. His breath ruffled the hair at the back of her neck as he growled out another question. "Do you want me?"

If she hadn't been on fire with need she would have rolled her eyes. What did he need, an engraved invitation? Okay, maybe he did. Maybe he wanted to be sure there wasn't any misunderstanding here. But if she hadn't been handcuffed, she might have been tempted to slug him. The delay was unbearable. "I thought only a vampire needed verbal permission to enter," she grumbled.

He vibrated against her with laughter. "Answer the question."

"Yes," she answered, thrusting back with her hips to make the message unmistakable.

"I'd stop if I could," he told her. "I wouldn't put you in danger willingly. I give you my protection, now and always."

Lou had a hazy moment to consider the potential hazards of werewolf sex and to wonder why he could possibly want to stop. The danger posed by the rogue werewolf seemed distant and unimportant. Still, his protective streak seemed kind of nice, really. He might not ever take her on a date or make the coffee in the morning, but he delivered a one-night stand with real flair.

Then he was thrusting into her, hard and deep, and the growing, thrumming thing inside her fed on it, getting stronger with each plunging stroke of his cock into her wet and aching cunt. And it still wasn't enough. She needed more, needed him to do something else.

Lou let out a fierce, wordless sound of need and demand. He responded, making his thrusts faster, slamming into her again and again. Power flooded her body in surges, each one stronger than the last, in time to his rhythmic thrusts. Just when she felt like her skin would split, it was too big to contain, he dug his fingers into her hips hard enough to bruise and impaled her with his thick cock in one final plunge.

She could feel his cock swelling even bigger and then spurting hot liquid deep into her core and that touched off both her own orgasm and the alien energy inside her. It was like shapeshifting but not quite the same. She kept her human form but felt an unmistakable sense of transformation taking place. It shook her entire being and drove the breath from her body.

Lou jerked helplessly under him, held fast by his hands, his body and his cock, caught in the throes of an unbelievably violent orgasm and something else that started somewhere in the center of her body and shot out in all directions as the power released. She wouldn't have been surprised to hear windshields shattering from the cars parked outside the bar. It didn't seem possible that a force like that, suddenly unleashed, could go unnoticed.

Chapter 3

What the hell was that? The question in her mind would have to wait until she found her voice again to ask it. Of course, maybe shapeshifter sex was always that intense. Lou wouldn't know—she hadn't had sex since her transformation. In fact, she hadn't had sex in far too long before that, now that she thought about it.

She thought about the months of celibacy stretching behind her when she could have had him fucking her mindless and wanted to cry at the waste, but she felt too relaxed, too giddy, too . . . drunk. As if the beer and Jell-O shot she'd had in the bar had contained something more potent than alcohol. That should have disturbed her, but she only wanted to roll against him and revel in the sensation of his bare skin against hers and imagine what it would be like to slide against his fur.

Something else should be disturbing her. Ah, yes, the liquid jet when he'd come inside her.

"You didn't use the condom," she said, but it wasn't an accusation. It came out slurred and disinterested.

"Didn't need ribbed or lubricated, did you?" He rubbed his cheek against her hair and then readjusted their position so they lay together spooned on their sides again, with his arms wrapped tight around her. He slid out of her in the process and Lou felt bereft.

"That's so wrong," she protested. "I need you back inside me."

"Told you you'd bitch if I didn't give you at least three orgasms."

He rolled onto his back and positioned her on top of him, facing him. She instantly spread her legs and scooted until the head of his cock nudged her cunt again. He was still thick and engorged, as ready for her as she was for him. With a little wiggle and a shift of angle, she had him sliding into her again. She made a soft sound of satisfaction.

He'd tugged her hair free of her ponytail at some point when she hadn't been paying attention and it fell over her shoulders in a silky slide when she moved. Although she was still wearing her bikini top, and that irritated her.

"Get this top off me," she muttered. "I need to rub my nipples on your chest."

"Your wish is my command." He undid the strings and slipped the top free. Lou closed her eyes in bliss as her bare breasts and her sensitized nipples came into solid contact with heated, male flesh.

She sighed and rubbed her cheek against him, luxuriating

in the feel of his body under her. "I want to rub all over you," she told him. "It's like I'm a cat and you're catnip. And I feel drunk. I thought I couldn't get drunk anymore. Tried a couple of times after I started turning furry. Didn't work. Metabolized all the alcohol too fast."

She licked at his skin, tasting the salty tang on her tongue, and wondered why she wanted to fill her mouth with him, wanted every orifice she had to contain him somehow. She mentioned this to him in a drunken slur and felt him finger her ass in response, circling her anus and then sliding a fingertip in.

That was better. His cock hard and thick inside her pussy, his finger teasing her ass. But that still left her mouth. Lou fastened her mouth onto his and sucked his tongue into hers. She wanted to suck his cock, but since she liked it far too much right where it was, she settled for letting him know with little growls and movements that she wanted his tongue fucking her mouth the way his cock was fucking her pussy while his fingertip fucked her ass.

She felt ravenous for him, and the feeling wasn't far removed from the animal bloodlust she'd begun to feel when the full moon approached. The need to hunt, to bring down her prey. Only now it was his sex she craved, and she craved it with her whole being.

And that made her realize that her animal side was rising into ascendance. Soon she wouldn't be able to hold off the change. The only thing keeping her in human form now was the fact that the beast inside her was being satiated by the animalistic mating they were engaged in.

Lou wondered vaguely if the key to werewolf control was

sex, if she could balance the beast and the human halves of herself by getting royally laid once a month, but it took too much effort to pursue any logical line of thought so she gave it up and focused on rocking her hips into his, sliding the length of his cock into her sex-starved sheath again and again.

This time it felt different in some way. She still needed his touch, his penetration, but she no longer felt like her skin couldn't contain the force contact between them created. It was still there, an invisible power running from him to her and back like a circuit, but tamer.

When she came again, shuddering and gasping against him, she didn't fear the distant sounds of shattering glass.

Drunk with pleasure and the sheer bliss of contact with him, Lou let herself collapse into him in a boneless heap. She let out a long, soft sigh of contentment.

"Mind if I finish?"

Oh. He was still hard inside her. "G'head," she murmured.

A few hard, quick thrusts and then she felt him spilling himself into her again. Her vaginal walls contracted sharply at the sensation and she quivered with the aftershocks of her orgasm and his.

After a seemingly endless time when she might have dozed, sated with sex and soothed by the rhythmic sounds of the surf and the drone of distant cars on the highway, his voice jolted her back to awareness.

"Okay. Now we need to talk."

Chapter 4

He was probably right, Lou mused. Conversations that started out that way weren't likely to end well. And it wasn't just the words *we need to talk* that set her mental alarm stirring. It was the tone of his voice, no longer tinged with laughter or amusement. He meant business now.

Well, all good things had to end. And at least he'd been true to his word and given her three orgasms first. She felt vaguely grateful to him for that even while annoyance at interrupting her post-coital bliss was rising up fast to counter it.

"Right, back to business," she sighed. "You're not the bad guy. I'm not the bad guy. Which means we should probably get dressed and go looking for him now."

"I meant we need to talk about other things," he told her. "Although that's certainly important too. How do you know I'm not the bad guy?"

"Dunno," she said. The line of logic that had told her he wasn't seemed too far away to grasp now. There had been something, though. What? Oh, yes. "You have a sense of humor," she pointed out.

"So do you. In a smart-ass kind of way." He let his hands rove away from her ass, which was unfortunate, and along her spine, which was nice enough that she forgave him. "Anything else?"

"It doesn't add up," she answered. "I figured out why, can't remember now. Gimme a minute."

That made him laugh. "I'll remember this, get you naked and handcuff you anytime I want to distract you. A few good orgasms and you're putty in my hands." He toyed with her hair. "You're not a natural blonde, are you?"

"Not telling." Lou smiled against his bare skin.

"I could make you tell me." One hand slid in between them so he could finger her still-sensitized clit.

Yeah, he certainly could. With that kind of torture, she'd sing like a canary. If she could talk. Problem was, coherent speech didn't really go along with what he was doing to her down there.

"But I'll find out soon enough. First things first. What's your name?"

"Louise. Lou," she clarified, figuring they were on intimate enough terms for him to use her nickname. The formality of having him use her full name after she'd asked him to bang her in the ass while fucking her would seem ludicrous. Not to mention hypocritical.

"Just Lou?"

"Catrell."

"Stuck on keeping the last name? Planning to hyphenate?"

"S' never come up," Lou informed him and wiggled her hips a little to get more pressure on her clit. A fourth orgasm didn't seem like a bad idea. Since she might never get another opportunity to play with him, it seemed only right to enjoy the present to the fullest.

But he was still focused on talking.

"It just did. I'm kind of a traditionalist, myself, always imagined my wife would take my last name. And I'd rather you didn't hyphenate, because that could lead to our kids having four last names someday."

Lou felt her eyes fly open at the implication. "Do you always propose to any girl who lets you handcuff her and do anal play on the first date?"

"We're a little past the proposal stage. We're mated. We consummated the bond. No condom, exchange of body fluids. I figured you'd prefer that to us drawing each other's blood in the act, by the way. For a werewolf, you seem kind of squeamish."

After a frozen moment, Lou discovered that she could in fact leap off him in spite of the handcuffs, the current dysfunctional state of her brain and the handicap of not really wanting to separate herself from his cock, not to mention his talented hands. She hit the sand, rolled and shook her head to clear it.

Clarity did not follow. "What? Excuse me?" she shrieked at him. "Are you saying we're *married*?"

"I asked you if you understood what was happening." He followed her, pinned her in the sand and scowled down at her. "You recognized me as your mate. What, does it mess with your plans that you can't fuck another male as long as I live?"

He didn't seem good-humored now. He seemed extremely pissed. She could feel the wolf inside him rising up and it didn't take much imagination to hear it snarling softly at her.

Whatever this mating business was, she knew instinctively that he was now her alpha as well as her mate and anything he perceived as a threat to deprive him of what he'd claimed territorially was a bad thing. She did not want that kind of a fight with him. Especially since he had the right to claim her, if she understood him correctly.

"Give me a minute," Lou managed to say. "This is a little surprising, okay? I need a moment to adjust. I came here hunting the big bad wolf. I wasn't planning a beachside wedding ceremony. Now you're telling me I just got married wearing nothing but a bikini top, sneakers and handcuffs."

She felt the full impact of that hit her. Then she smacked her head into the sand. Hard. Repeatedly. "Not a Kodak moment. Okay? Most women get apple blossoms, white lace, that kind of thing. And I could be wrong, but I'm pretty sure Jan and Dean never performed 'The Wedding March.'"

"Oh." The tension went out of him. He touched her face lightly. "I can see how this lacks a little in the way of romance from your perspective. We could go to Vegas, have a strictly human ceremony if you like."

"Because getting married to a total stranger in a neon chapel by a guy dressed like Elvis would be so much better? I don't even know your *name*." Lou felt her lips tremble, heard the betraying quaver in her voice and felt tears well up in her eyes. Oh, hell, now she was going to top off the evening by crying like a girl. If she'd spent the last year planning ways to screw tonight up, she couldn't have beat this.

"It's Dylan."

"Dylan," she repeated. She sniffled. "Dylan the werewolf?" That was funny enough to head off the unwanted weeping fit.

"My mom was into poetry," he informed her. "Dylan Thomas, Bob Dylan. I suffered for it. But I didn't get turned into a werewolf until I was eighteen, so it's not like she knew I was going to grow up to lead a wolf pack."

"Guess not. I'm sure my mom never imagined my current life, either."

He bent forward and brushed his lips across hers gently. The kiss was sweet and reassuring. Unrushed, undemanding, it seduced her into wanting more. Only a kiss, but her body flooded with heat while her vaginal walls flooded with liquid and clenched reflexively in anticipation. "There's a human life too."

"Right." Lou thrashed in the sand until she had herself cuddled into Dylan. He accommodated her, wrapping arms and legs around her and snuggling her close. The more of him she was in contact with, the better she felt. Touching him was an irresistible compulsion. It comforted her and made her feel safe. Warm. Secure. Even, weirdly, loved. "How come I want to keep touching you?"

"We're mated. The bond is new. We feed it by touch."

Well, there was an answer. Sort of. But she could find out more about that later. Now it seemed more important to learn a little more about the man she'd gotten herself bound to. "So what are you doing here in California, anyway? You're not from around here."

"I got transferred."

The utter normalcy of that floored her. He had a day job. Chances were, his coworkers had no idea what he did during the full moon.

"Didn't somebody else used to be alpha before you got here?" Lou asked. "What happened, a fight to the death?"

Dylan laughed. "Hardly. He wanted to retire. His mate wanted to move to the Florida Keys to live on a houseboat. So I made them both happy and took over the local pack." He grinned at her. "Not very dramatic."

"And what do you do when you're not howling at the moon?"

"I'm a system administrator."

Lou nodded. "That works. Those guys are all weird, you'd fit right in."

"And what about you? What do you do when you're not picking up strange men in bars?"

"I used to be in insurance claims."

"Used to be?"

"I quit when I realized I wanted to tear my boss's throat out for refusing to cover a kid's cancer treatment." Lou brooded for a moment. "I wasn't sure if I'd actually do it one night when I wasn't exactly myself, so I figured a little distance was in order. And it gave me more time to focus on revenge. You know, hunting down the rabid jerk who turned me into Ms. Most In Need of Electrolysis once a month."

"Ah. So that's how you ended up a werewolf who doesn't know what happens when you meet your mate. You weren't a planned addition to a pack, you were a victim of a rogue attack." He sat up and pulled her upright with him in a fluid motion. "That explains what you were doing in the bar tonight. I thought at first you might've been an accomplice."

"So you handcuffed me and gave me the best sex of my life anyway?"

"He might have coerced you into helping if he was your alpha. So I gave you the opportunity to change allegiances," he explained. "By the time we got to the sex part, I'd figured out you weren't with him. Our wolves recognized each other as mates. Best sex in your life?"

"Maybe only the second best." Lou kept a straight face and gave him a considering look. "Maybe I need another round to see how you rate."

"You're an animal." He gave her a slow, feral smile that told her how much he liked that about her.

"Any time now," Lou agreed. "I can't believe I'm still wearing skin instead of fur. It's late."

"The mating bond," he nodded. "We started in human form, we had to remain in that form until it was complete."

"Isn't it complete now?"

"Yes, but there are aftereffects. Do you actually know anything about werewolves that you didn't learn from comic books or movies?"

"Yeah, I got a real education in an alley one night," she shot back. "Okay, so I'm dumb about the wolf stuff. You can bring me up to speed. It's not like the one who tried to kill me hung around to see if I'd changed and needed a mentor."

"Don't be touchy." He pressed his thumb against her lips

in a half-caress, half-silencing gesture. "I should probably mention the no condom thing again now. Most couples hope for pregnancy as a result of the ritual. Children conceived during mating have special abilities. It's considered a blessing on the bonded pair. If I'd realized you didn't know anything, I would have acted differently. I couldn't have stopped, once mates recognize each other mating can't be stopped. But I could've used the condom."

"So I could be knocked up right now and we could be the proud parents of something out of the X-Men? You know, I don't think most one-night stands are this complicated." Lou closed her eyes and buried her face in the curve of his neck.

"It might not happen."

"No, it'd be just my luck to have twins. You haven't even had a chance to see me at my best and you'll be watching me hurl for the next nine months, blowing up like a blimp and then screaming through labor. Just what every fledgling relationship needs."

Dylan scooped her into his lap and placed a kiss on top of her bleached-blond hair. "On the bright side, this is truly 'til death do us part. I'll never desire any other female above you. I wouldn't leave you. And we'll never stop needing to touch each other, although in a week or so we'll be able to leave each other long enough to go about a normal life, going to work, that kind of thing. But mates don't separate, not without becoming seriously weakened, and if it goes on too long it's fatal."

"So no going home to Mother if I get mad at you."

"Nope. We fight it out and stay together." He nuzzled her playfully. "And then we have make-up sex."

"Which the twins will interrupt just when it's getting good."

"Are you always this grumpy? Or are you still pissed about getting married in nothing but sneakers and handcuffs?"

"And a bikini top," Lou reminded him. "I think that adds a touch of class."

"I need a real answer here." He tipped her chin up and made eye contact. "I need to know you don't regret this. My entire adult life I've known the wolf in me would recognize my mate. It's something I accepted long ago. To resist is to fight against your own nature. That doesn't happen often among us, but when it does, the results are unhappy to say the least. It's not enough that you belong to me now. I need you to want to be mine. I want all of you."

And the weird part was, she believed him. Maybe it was another effect of their mating, maybe it created a sort of emotional resonance or empathy, because she could feel the tension in him, feel him willing her to want him, to . . . love him.

It mattered to him that she was there willingly, that she wanted to be his and that he would hold her heart as well as her body.

Their wolves had recognized each other as mates, he'd said. And in the past year she'd learned to trust her wolf self. It had never led her wrong. It frequently led her away from trouble her human self would never have seen coming.

She'd known him for only a few hours.

She was probably certifiably insane.

But she was pretty sure she did, in fact, love him. The term he'd used, recognition, really did describe what she felt.

It was as if her wolf self recognized him, remembered him and was making her human body and her heart remember too. Almost as if they'd known each other before in some other realm, where they'd run together under a distant sky, hunted together, depended on each other, mated for all time.

Lou opened her mouth to tell him what he needed to hear, but before she could, an inhuman howl split the night.

Chapter 5

They've spotted him," Dylan said. He reached for his jeans, retrieved the key to the handcuffs and freed her. "My pack's been watching this place, waiting for him. We can't allow a rogue to go free, and we can't leave him to human justice. Stay here. I'll call you when it's safe."

Call her when it was safe? Leave her behind while the men took care of business? That seemed like a bad precedent. But he slid into his jeans and vanished into the darkness before she could argue with him.

"Dammit," Lou muttered. She groped in the sand for her bikini, found it and scrambled into it. All she needed to do now was retrieve her gun to complete the Terminator Barbie look.

How was Dylan planning to take the bad guy out, anyway? He wasn't armed. She would have smelled the gun oil if he'd had one, which was why she'd left hers in the car. She knew she wouldn't have a chance of getting up close and personal with the big, bad wolf without him knowing she was packing and she'd needed to appear helpless to attract him. The gun would have given away the game. Since killing his victims in their cars seemed like his favorite way to get his jollies, hiding the gun in her glove box had struck Lou as the perfect solution.

Oh, shit. Dylan was going to fight him. Lou felt icy fear prickle along her spine. And he might not be able to shift yet because of the aftereffects holding their transformation off. He might even now be facing a rogue werewolf in his too-vulnerable human form.

She retrieved her jacket with the car keys and ran to her car, grateful every step of the way for the strength and speed she'd gained along with her wolf self. If she'd been merely human, she wouldn't have been fast enough. She reached the car, shoved in the key and turned it just as the sounds of fighting reached her ears. One punch on the button to her glove box and then the Springfield Armory compact was in her hand. She grabbed it and checked the chamber as she ran to make sure the round was still there. Counting the round in the chamber, she had eight shots. It would have to be enough.

Of course, if eight .45 caliber hollow-point rounds didn't stop the rogue werewolf, finding more bullets would be the least of their problems. Lou refused to think that she'd be such a rotten shot at the critical moment that all eight bullets would miss. Her new abilities included better than human vision and reflexes. Her aim had been honed on the practice range until she was confident in her ability to shoot straight when the target was moving, and accuracy and speed mattered.

I won't miss, she chanted silently while she ran. *I'll nail that bastard and Dylan will be fine. He won't be hurt.* And then added in a silent prayer for help to any power listening, *please.*

Lou could hear them before she could see them, her sensitive ears locating sources of movement in the night. She could only hope the good guys wouldn't think she was part of the problem and attack her while she found a place to take aim.

Then she could see them, her mate and the rogue. Two massive wolves locked in combat while the other weres ranged around them. Maybe it was an aftereffect of mating, but she knew Dylan even in his wolf form instantly. He'd been able to shift, after all, while she remained locked in human form. Maybe because he was stronger than she was, maybe because he knew more than she did or had better control. Whatever the reason, she was grateful for her hands and more aware than ever of the urgent need to use them before they turned to paws.

The combatants tumbled together, a flurry of snapping jaws and lightning-fast movements. No clear shot. She couldn't be sure she wouldn't hit Dylan until they separated.

The rogue wolf was huge, powerful and not bound by any sense of decency to fight fair or any hesitation to do mortal injury. And Lou doubted he was burdened much by sanity. Given the abnormal feats of strength an insane human was capable of, what could an insane werewolf do? She didn't doubt Dylan's strength or agility, but she also didn't trust anything short of a silver bullet to stop this monster. Fear for her mate rose up but she ruthlessly forced it down. No time for that now. Now what mattered was watching for her moment and taking it when it came.

Dylan broke free for an instant and whirled to take a new angle of attack. The rogue followed, but it was all the opportunity she needed, a clear shot with no other werewolves behind him. That mattered. The hollow-point bullets would stop on impact, but the silver filling they carried was another story. There was a risk the silver would continue on through the body and out the other side, endangering any werewolf unlucky enough to get in the way. Lou aimed for his head, told herself she was just at the range shooting another practice target and pulled the trigger.

The sound hurt her ears but she didn't flinch. She kept the gun steady and followed the first shot with the rest of the clip in rapid succession.

She didn't miss. The rogue werewolf shifted into a naked man as he fell to the ground.

"Eat silver, you bastard," Lou said out loud in satisfaction. "I might have learned about werewolves from comic books and movies, but they got that part right."

Then she dropped the gun and ran to her mate.

She got a fierce growl instead of thanks.

"Yes, I know. I was supposed to wait." She flung her arms around Dylan's neck and hugged him to her, needing the contact to reassure herself that he was unhurt. "You should know right from the start that I'm not going to sit back and twiddle my thumbs like some useless decoration when you need me."

Then the transfiguring touch of the full moon told Lou that the time for words had ended. Tomorrow they could talk again.

She shifted into her second form while Dylan waited. Then they ran together in the night, running for the sheer physical joy of it, side by side, pacing each other, sharing the wild night that stretched out before them, and it was like coming home.

"So you're not a natural blonde."

The teasing words chased away the last remnants of sleep. Lou came awake and turned her head to find the speaker. She opened her eyes to see a pair of amber eyes gazing down at her. Laugh lines crinkled in the corners, deepened by the satisfied smile that currently filled Dylan's face. He was obviously pleased with himself for guessing right.

She vaguely remembered that they'd made their way to his home in the predawn dark and fallen into bed together as they shifted back to human form. By the angle of the sun streaming through the window, she guessed it was close to noon now.

"Nope," Lou agreed, smiling back at him. "Clairol trumps Mother Nature."

"Want to tell me where you got silver bullets? You can't just buy those off the shelf."

"Nope," she said again. "And even asking questions about them will get you some pretty strange looks, in case you wondered. Amazing how anybody wanting to know about silver bullets comes off as a whack job." She reached out to touch his bare chest, letting her hand trail down to his abdomen in a lingering caress. The need to touch him would probably lessen over time, but she didn't think it would ever go away. "I settled for regular hollow-points and filled them with silver myself. Very carefully."

"Effective." Dylan captured her wayward hand with one of his and carried it to his mouth. He pressed a kiss into her palm. "You're a good shot too. Remind me not to piss you off."

"Don't piss me off," Lou said, fighting the urge to giggle. One night with him and she felt downright lighthearted, happy, buoyant. Pissed off seemed like an impossibility at the moment.

"But as the alpha around here, if you disobey me again you'll find yourself back in handcuffs."

"Promises, promises."

Lou was pretty sure he'd keep them though. And was looking forward to it.

Stolen Goddess

TAWNY TAYLOR

Chapter 1

Kylie Mannings hated Saturday nights. They reminded her of things she'd just as soon forget, like the time she'd gotten so drunk she'd tripped over a crack in the sidewalk and broken her ankle. Or the time she'd gotten a speeding ticket from a good-looking cop who had no appreciation for the risks of being late for a night of club-hopping with the girls. Or Adam Hubbard, the tall, dark-haired hunk of manliness she'd recently made an ex-boyfriend.

Yeah, Saturday nights sucked.

The ankle had eventually healed. And after paying AAA an atrocious amount for approximately thirty-six months for car insurance, along with a tidy sum to the city, the ticket fiasco was finally over. But the final issue—that of said ex-boyfriend—was still fresh in a "life sucks" kind of way. The kicker—it shouldn't have happened.

In this day and age, Kylie figured, a girl shouldn't have to choose between wedded bliss and a career. It was only her luck that she'd dated a guy who would put her in precisely that position—where she'd have to choose. He'd done that, and in the end they'd both lost. Big time.

As much as she liked Adam, just up and moving to the other side of the world wasn't possible now, not with her career finally taking the turn she'd hoped for. Years of planning were at stake. Planning and hard work, not to mention some serious ass-kissing.

This was not just any little promotion. This was a once-in-a-lifetime promotion. Starting Monday morning she was vice president! Vice president of Sales and Marketing for a fastener manufacturer who catered to, or more like indulged, the Big Three. Anyone who knew the automotive industry knew how unlikely it was for a woman to end up in a position more powerful than office manager. A more likely position was legs spread, flat on her back under the other three vice presidents of the company. Somehow, by some small miracle, she'd sidestepped the first and avoided the latter.

In all honesty, Kylie expected to see a flock of pigs flying south at any moment.

The fact that it was Halloween and she was home alone, sitting on her front porch and waiting for kids who didn't seem to be coming didn't help her glum mood at all. Six feet four, two hundred twenty pounds of sin wrapped in Tommy Hilfiger, Adam had always made a big deal out of every holiday. But Halloween was his all-time favorite. Last year, he'd made her dress up as Eve—of biblical fame. Together, sporting matching felt fig leaves, they'd handed out bucketloads of candy to trick-or-treaters, and later went party-hopping before returning home to enjoy hours of sex.

How things had changed in one year! She sure as hell wasn't going to get any sex this year.

She missed Adam, even though she knew she hadn't loved him. While their sex life had rocked, there'd been something missing in the emotion department. Not that she had reason to complain. Her lack of deeper feelings had made it easy to keep their relationship casual. Casual was good. Casual didn't interfere in plans, careers.

Not happy about the direction her thoughts were headed, she shook her head, like it would knock those unhappy thoughts away, glanced at her watch for the umpteenth time—in twenty minutes—and wrapped her jacket tighter around herself. The wind had picked up and gusts of arctic air were slapping her cheeks and tossing her hair. Her nose and fingers were growing numb, fast. So was her butt, thanks to the fact that her porch was the size of a postage stamp and wouldn't accommodate a chair. It was amazing how cold concrete got.

This was stupid. Lame. Pathetic. So what if she'd planned for this night for weeks? Shopped the candy sales. Picked up all the "good" candy so the kids would beam with joy. Why couldn't she just admit that sometimes plans didn't work out, and move on?

After checking up and down her street for signs of little fairies, devils or dragons, she reluctantly picked up the bowl of candy and headed inside. No reason to sit outside on the porch and freeze like a dork with no life. She had a life. She had a career. And she had things to do, besides sitting in the cold and risking frostbite on her ass. She left the porch light on in case any kids did wander her way, and threw herself on the couch with a book. Not quite a chapter into her reading, the doorbell rang for the first time.

Although she had determined ages ago that she was not mother material—hand in hand with kids came chaos, she'd seen it with her friends—she still adored handing out candy to cute kiddies in costumes on Halloween. Glad to finally have some visitors, she scooped up fistfuls of wrapped chocolate bars, donned a "Happy Halloween" smile and threw open the door to greet them.

The minute she opened the door she had a funny feeling. The kids standing on the other side weren't your typical trick-or-treaters. There were two of them, dressed head-to-toe in black. They towered over her by at least six inches. Probably outweighed her by a hundred pounds each.

They sure were making kids big these days.

"What do your mothers feed you?" she asked, smiling despite a swelling sense of doom. "Whole cows?" Prepared to dole out the Snickers bars melting in her fists, she looked down at their hands. That was when she realized they were not trick-or-treating. Instead of pillowcases loaded with suckers and Twix, these guys were holding rope.

Out of sheer instinct, she threw the candy—not that a half-dozen Snickers would hurt a couple of giant thugs—jumped backward and swung the door, but it was too late, they were inside and on top of her before she could scream, "I have Mace."

Thanks to a significant size and strength disparity, and the fact that she had been lying and had no Mace, she lost the wrestling match pretty quickly. She also lost something else, thanks to a smelly rag smashed up against her mouth and nose.

She lost consciousness.

"You'll have to be punished," someone said. Someone male. Someone close. Someone with an extremely deep voice. She liked deep voices. And punishment didn't always have to be a bad thing.

Anxious to see who was promising discipline with the deep bass voice, despite the pounding in her head, Kylie dragged her eyelids up, uncovering eyes that felt like they'd been rolled in sand. Everything was still very hazy. Dark. Strange. She felt groggy, sick, like she'd overdosed on Nyquil. She tried to sit up but realized she couldn't. Her hands were tied up over her head. While wriggling her arms, she tested her feet. They too were tied.

What the fuck?

She could see there were only two people in the tiny room—her and the man who had spoken. He was completely nude. Nude and sporting a hard-on that suggested he was quite happy to see her, yet he glared at her, rage pulling his features into a tense mask. Oh boy. This was not good. Was he going to rape her?

A girl who'd lived in some rough neighborhoods growing up, she went into survival mode—decided pretty quickly she'd better go easy with this guy, try to gain his trust. She'd soothe his ruffled feathers. Pretend to go along with whatever he wanted until she found the opportunity to escape. He looked furious. And he looked strong. At the moment, she was not in the ideal position to defend herself. Yes, playing the waiting game was definitely in order.

However, her carefully laid plans changed when a quick glance down verified what she'd suspected almost immediately after waking—she was naked.

Embarrassment and shame swept through her body, churning in her belly with a good amount of anger. What right did this guy have? Taking her from her home, stripping her, holding her hostage! It was downright . . . medieval! No, it was cavemanish. She should be the one glowering. Despite her fear about the consequences, she gave the Neanderthal a glare right back.

"I can see your attitude hasn't improved yet," he said sharply.

"Huh? Yet? How would you know about my attitude? You've never seen it before." She had to get out of there. Now. She gritted her teeth and yanked at the rope holding her wrists.

"Of course I've seen this attitude before." Something flashed through his eyes. "How dare you lie to me!"

"Lie?" Was this guy nuts? Or was this some kind of sick game? "You couldn't have seen my attitude before because we've never met. I have no idea who you are or what I'm doing strapped to this fucking bed, naked. How dare *you*!"

Whatever he was going to say—and she knew he was about to speak because he'd opened his mouth—got caught somewhere between his chest and tongue. He snapped his jaw shut and, turning, threw open a door.

The two thugs who'd masqueraded as trick-or-treaters stepped inside. The three of them—the Thug Brothers and the Neanderthal—huddled together, whispering, pointing, nodding collective heads. Then they stalked toward her.

She had to say, she quickly gained a new appreciation for how turkeys felt on Thanksgiving Day.

Despite the fact that the bindings holding her wrists and ankles were tighter than bear traps, she fought them fiercely. As a result of her frenzied yanking and thrashing, the rope burned her skin, cutting deeply until she had to stop. She was worn out and a victim of agonizing pain, after only a few minutes of struggling and a couple shallow burns. Sad. She was a wimp! How would she ever get out of this alive? She vowed to get back to the gym if she lived through this ordeal.

Her bare breasts rose and fell with each racing gasp. Her wrists were killing her. Her heart was heavy with the knowledge that she was entirely at the men's mercies. Yet she refused to acknowledge defeat. Still breathless and totally embarrassed by her nudity, she scraped up what was left of her pride, lifted her chin and stared the tallest one—the Neanderthal—right in the eyes.

To hell with placating him! She felt as raw as her wrists. Her emotions were taking over, clouding her thoughts. Anger. Fear. Confusion.

That had never happened to her before. That confused her more.

"I am certain this is her. But she insists—"

"Of course it's her," Thug Brother One said, pointing at the tattoo she had on her hip bone. The design was one-of-a-kind, an intricate series of swirls and curlicues she'd dreamed about once a long time ago and had sketched a bazillion times after. In notebooks, on scrap paper, in her address book. "She has the mark."

"Mark? That's just a doodle," she said. "My doodle. No one else has ever seen it before." Just her luck, they thought it was some kind of brand or something.

"We checked before bringing her," Thug Brother Two said, nodding.

The asshole holding her hostage nodded and let the men out, then turned, his jaw set.

She'd seen many a man with that expression before. Men who were determined to sink a putt, or close a deal, no matter what. As much as she hated to admit it, it was an expression that had turned her on in the past, especially when she'd seen it on Adam's mug. A shameful thing, but here too it had an effect on her. The firm set of the Neanderthal's jaw had her squirming, even though she had no idea who he was or what he wanted with her.

It was time to be honest with herself, she decided, since she could very well be facing some life-altering events, if not life-ending. Despite her shock, anger and fear, she hadn't been able to ignore the Neanderthal's shocking good looks. This guy was straight out of her fantasies, right down to the dark curly hair that was a little too long to be fashionable. Physically, he was a combination of all her favorite movie stars. Vin Diesel's body. Antonio Banderas's coloring and hair. A touch of Orlando Bloom. She'd never in a million years dreamed of getting busy with a guy who looked as good as that, like he'd walked off a movie set. This guy made Andy—er, Adam!—look like dog meat.

"You say you don't remember me. So, I guess I have no other choice." He stood next to her, too close. His gaze smoothed up and down her body like a sensual caress.

"I didn't say I don't remember you. I said I've never met . . . you . . ." She felt herself melting. Her body's instantaneous reaction pissed her off and she was forced to explain it away in a rush of empty excuses to maintain her self-respect. Kylie Mannings was a strong woman. A woman with a backbone. A mind. She did not appreciate being treated like a brainless hunk of prime rib laid out on a hibachi. He stared at her breasts and her nipples tingled, sending little zaps of wanting down her spine. "Urgh!"

Yes, she had a mind. Even if her tongue was tied in knots at the moment and she was talking like a Neanderthal.

"I'll simply have to reacquaint us," he said, sounding — and looking — downright pleased. He licked his lips. She stared. He had nice lips. Full for a guy. They looked soft. Yummy. He leaned closer and ran a single fingertip down the center of her belly.

Even as she shuddered with desire, she growled, "Like hell you will. Don't you dare touch me or I'll scream. Loud."

His chuckle sent shivers through her body, good shivers, the kind she hadn't indulged in since Adam left. And the smile, well, that nearly put her in a coma. "I must say, I've never seen this side of you. You've always been such a . . . compliant wife."

Her tongue sprung free of its knot. "What? Wife? Did you say wife?" she interrupted. Why would he think she was his wife? Was that what he was saying? No. She'd misunderstood. There could be no other explanation.

He frowned. She had to admit, the smile did a lot more for her than the frown. "Yes, of course I said wife," he said. "We've been married for almost six years." He leaned forward, closer, closer, closer, until his breath warmed her lips. He was going to kiss her? He thought she was his wife. Shouldn't she try to correct him before he did something crazy, like lay those lips on hers? Yes. Yes, she should. "Don't you remember me?" he asked. He blew a cool stream of air on her mouth and a rush of warmth blazed along her nerves. She closed her eyes and sucked in a gasp. "We've been very, very happily married," he added. His lips brushed gently across hers in a light, teasing kiss. "Until you left."

Her resolve crumbled. They'd figure out all that wife stuff later.

"Why'd you leave me?" he asked.

Good question.

"I know everything about you," he continued. "Like how you love me to pinch your nipples . . ." While she lay shamefully still, he closed a forefinger and thumb over each taut bud and squeezed until she was near tears and her heart was skipping beats and her pussy was wet and hot and ready. ". . . like this and then kiss them." He leaned over her and closed his warm mouth over one still-stinging nub, taking away the pain with slow, lazy swipes of his velvety tongue.

Oh, she wasn't lying so still any longer. But she wasn't exactly trying to get away, either.

His hand cupped her other breast, kneading its softness and teasing the nipple until she was begging for relief, until cream was making her pussy slick and she was writhing under him. Hot, tense, wanting.

This was insanity! She'd never had sex with a stranger. Not even when she was stupid-drunk in college and everyone around her was hopping in the sack with whomever they could get their hands on. She'd always been careful, thought things out before she'd slept with a new lover. Not even Adam had been able to get past her defenses the first night— though he did try! She'd made the poor man wait almost a full month before she'd given in. She could just imagine how many nights he'd walked into his house, nursing a set of aching testicles from the tormenting she'd given them.

But, oh, the agony she was facing now! Her pussy was burning up. Empty. Her body was aching for completion she instinctively knew only this man could give her. She trembled with need. This wasn't just her average need. This was need beyond words.

Would it be so wrong to have sex with this man?

She shook away the thought, rocked her head from side to side. Why was she even considering this now? It made no sense. He'd had her kidnapped! Sure, he was under the false impression that she was his wife. So really, in his eyes, he'd just paid a couple of thugs to get his wife back. Was that kidnapping? Perhaps he'd thought she was in trouble.

"I know how you love to play chasing games. Is that why you left? Was it another game?" His expression changed, from confusion to wicked pleasure. "That's what it was, wasn't it? You were waiting for me to find you. Discipline you." He traced a circle around one nipple with an index finger then drew little wavering lines on her lower belly. "You're so naughty. I want to fuck you."

Oh, God! Why was her pussy clenching around its own

heated emptiness? Her hips rocking back and forth in time with the waves of wanting crashing through her body? This wasn't her husband.

Actually, she knew why, but she wasn't ready to accept it yet.

He left her side and walked around the foot of the bed to kneel on the mattress and wedge his knees between her legs. She dropped her head back and tightened her spine with anticipation. She couldn't look at him, couldn't watch as his gaze traveled her length, settled at the thick patch of curls between her thighs, slick with the evidence of her need. He set his hands on her knees then slowly slid them higher, up her thighs until they rested on either side of her hips and his thumbs were dipping into the sensitive creases on either side of her center. "Only I know what makes you wet. What makes you tremble with desire. What makes you beg for more."

That was it. Her brain raised the white flag, admitting defeat. Now she was ready to accept why she was considering sleeping with this man, this . . . stranger.

What he said was true, somehow he knew her. Oh, yes he did. At least he knew her body. He knew how to touch her, where to touch her. He knew how ticklish she was, how a kiss just above her pubic bone made her squirm. How a stroke to the sensitive skin at the backs of her knees would make her beg for more. What to say to make her tremble.

Could she be wrong about not knowing him? Had they met somewhere? Made love? How could that be?

When he dragged his tongue over her folds, she decided she didn't give a damn how it could be. She'd sort it all out later.

For once in her life, Kylie Mannings would act on a whim. She'd forget about plans and consequences. She'd follow her heart. Just this once. To hell with logic.

As if he sensed her acquiescence, he stopped the tender loving care he was so generously lavishing on her pussy and untied her feet. She was beyond thrilled when he gently forced her knees to bend and pushed them back until her pussy was wide open for him. Oh, yes, it felt so good. So right. She moaned.

"That's it, love. Turn yourself over to me. Let yourself go."

She couldn't do anything but. There wasn't a nerve ending that wasn't tingling. There wasn't a muscle fiber that wasn't pulled tight. There wasn't a sensation that wasn't amplified to the extreme—smell, taste, touch. She was drowning in a blissful sea of sounds and touches and scents. She could hear the sharp intake of breath when she tipped her hips to silently plead for more. She could feel the cool, smooth texture of the sheets underneath her. And the spicy, all-male scent of him was making her dizzy. Like an addict, she kept dragging in deep breaths through her nose, wishing the smell would linger there, where she could enjoy it forever.

His tongue found her clit and danced over it in a series of swift flickers that had her bucking and pleading and panting. She was so hot, burning up from head to toe, like from a fever. It was too much, yet not enough. She wanted it to end, the torture. And she wanted it to go on forever.

"Fuck me," she begged. She wrapped her fingers around the rope and squeezed. The rough fibers scratched her palms but the slight pain only amplified the pleasure. "Please, oh please. Fuck me."

"Very well, wife." His voice was low, gritty, and she guessed he was as desperate for completion as she was.

She nearly wept with gratitude when a few stuttering heartbeats later she felt him kneel at her bottom, lift her hips and prod at her pussy with his cock. He didn't thrust in quickly, like most guys who slept with her did. Oh no, this guy was going for the major climax. He buried himself slowly, inch by glorious inch. It was delicious torture. She trembled. She threw her head from side to side. She couldn't help it; she moaned.

"Yes, my naughty wife. How you love to be punished." Now firmly seated in her vagina, his cock felt huge. Thick and long and absolutely perfect. Tears stung her eyes. Tears from what, she had no idea. No, maybe she did have a little bit of an idea. For some reason, she felt like she'd come home, like she'd found the man she'd been missing for a long, long time.

His withdrawal was just as slow and agonizing as his entry and it did everything to stir her lust to new heights. Whereas with every other man she'd always been after the Big O, with this one she didn't want it to be over. Yet she felt her body racing toward the finish line, without any help from her mind. In fact, she was trying to resist it, yet she couldn't.

Powerless. Completely out of control, of even her own body. And oh, so happy! What was going on?

Was it the ropes? Was it the wicked promises he whispered in her ear as he fell into a slow but steady pattern of thrusts with that wonderful cock of his? Was it the fact that she didn't even know his name?

He leaned lower, until his lightly haired chest brushed

against her erect nipples. It tickled and she gasped in surprise. "Yes, that's it, love. Let yourself go. Give it all to me, everything you are, everything you think and feel and need. It's all mine now. You are mine."

Insane or not, at the moment she could think of nothing but being his, in every way. "Oh, God," she heard herself mutter. She tipped her hips to meet his thrusts, deepen them. She loved the way his cock glided in and out, caressing that special spot inside her, the one that sent waves of liquid heat crashing through her body. She blinked open her eyes, not even sure she remembered closing them. Her gaze met his. It was fierce, yet she sensed a tenderness churning below the surface. Hot and demanding, but also kind and loving.

"Who are you?" she asked, letting her eyelids fall closed again. He was too close, it was all too intense. A part of her wanted to hide while another wanted to bare everything, all her fears, disappointments. Doubts.

He stilled for a moment, leaving his cock deep inside her. "I'm anyone you want me to be. Your refuge." He kissed her forehead. "Your protector." He kissed her left eye and then her right. "Your friend." He kissed her chin. "Your Master." He slanted his mouth over hers in a kiss so gentle yet thorough she felt like she'd died and gone to heaven.

When he resumed his steady thrusts, she *knew* she'd died and gone to heaven.

Her climax swept over her like a tsunami, throwing her into a world of pulsing, heated wetness where nothing existed but the man on top of her. She heard him shout his release, felt his cock thicken and his thrusts quicken as he pumped his seed deep inside her.

Afterward, he pulled out, untied her, rolled onto his side and held her sweetly in his arms. He kissed the angry red welts on her wrists then dragged one hand down the length of her hair, plucking up a lock and holding it to his nose to inhale.

"What is this scent? It's so sweet, yet nutty. Is it from that strange world where Brothers Rido and Ikuni found you?"

"Strange world? It's just coconut. And it didn't come from a *world*, it came from a bottle. Suave, as a matter of fact. Hardly something beyond the common American's reach."

"American." He sighed. "I wish you could take me to this world you visit. I would very much like to see it." He nuzzled her neck, his whiskers stirring up a serious case of goose bumps. "Such smells. I can only imagine what sights you've seen. I talked to the Wise One. He told me about . . . about you. About your world. Tried to explain why you had to leave. I don't understand it all," he growled. "He told me I shouldn't have brought you back. But I couldn't stand it, dammit . . . I missed you. I had to have you back. You are my wife. Mine. He had no right taking you away from me."

Even though Kylie didn't know this guy, she sensed his sadness, his desperation to reach her. Who was his wife? And why had she left? And why did he think she was his wife? And who was this Wise One? And what did she make of all this talk about "her world"? She tipped her head to look at his face. He looked rumpled and adorable and sated. But also sad. Like he'd lost his best friend.

Oh, man.

She had to tell him the truth. Somehow. She was a complete jerk for not driving her point home earlier, instead of allowing him to drive his, quite literally. But now that her hormones were in check, the gag had been loosened from the voice of her conscience. "Listen, we need to talk about this 'wife' thing," she began. Not sure how to continue, she sat up and wrapped a blanket around herself.

He caught her hand in his and gave her a sharp gaze. "I won't let you leave again. No. Tell me I have no right to ask about your leaving, and I will accept it, only because you are our Goddess. But you will always be mine." He dragged his fingers through his hair. The motion set the muscles of his arm and shoulder rippling. It was some sight. "I wish you could talk to me about these things. I . . . I understand why you can't. I've known for a long time there would be a time—I mean, being the Goddess, you are forced to—"

"The goddess?" she repeated, so incredibly lost. Where was this conversation going? He thought she was his wife. He thought she was a goddess? A goddess who had left for some purpose he didn't know and had no right to ask about? This whole thing sounded like the plot of some B-grade sci-fi film. Nervous, she stood, dragging the blanket off the bed.

"What is it? What do you need? I'll call for your maids." The man—her lover, supposed husband, whatever—scrambled over the bed and pulled a cord at the head. It was interesting, how he'd changed since they'd had sex. Before, he'd been so forceful, so sexy and self-assured and strong. Now there was something else there, a little bit of uncertainty, which only added to her confusion. It also made her feel really, really guilty.

She firmed up her resolve and looked him dead in the eye. "Okay. Last time. I'm not your wife. I'm certainly no goddess, unless you're talking about the goddess of disasters, because that I will accept. And I'm extremely sorry for taking advantage of the situation and having sex with you, thereby letting you think I was indeed your wife. Now, if you don't mind, I'm going to head home, have a glass, or two, or maybe a bottle, of wine to help me forget all about this—not that it was all bad, mind you," she said, wanting to spare his male pride. "But I had no right and I'd better go. I need to get ready for Monday." When he didn't say anything, she accepted that as his acceptance that her leaving was best, and headed for the door.

It was unlocked but she didn't step outside. No sooner did she open the door than she halted, agape, and even more confused than she'd been not ten seconds earlier. Standing before her were not one, not two, but three women. Three women with the same blonde hair that wasn't straight or curly. Three women with the same features that weren't ugly but weren't exactly beautiful, either. Three women with the same body, fair-skinned and barely covered in matching outfits that looked like bejeweled bikinis.

They were, in fact, all three mirror images. Exact replicas . . . of herself!

Chapter 2

W ife, if I must, I'll tie you to the bed again," came that gravelly male voice from somewhere behind Kylie. "You haven't yet had your punishment. You will not leave me again."

Stunned, she staggered. Her shoulder smacked into the door frame. Her gaze hopped from one shockingly familiar face to the next like a grasshopper on crack. Her three clones eyed her with curiosity for a split second before literally dropping to their knees at her feet.

"What is it you wish of us?" asked Clone Number One, her forehead practically resting on Kylie's big toe.

"We live to serve you," said Clone Number Two.

"Our Goddess," said Clone Number Three. "We did not know you had returned."

"Wife! Return to me," demanded the nearly forgotten man in the room behind her.

Kylie took a moment to steady herself, both literally and figuratively. For some reason, everyone around here—wherever here was, she'd yet to figure that one out—thought she was a goddess. Royalty—no, *deity*. They looked like they were literally worshipping her feet. It was creepy. She'd never been a deity before—at least, not outside her own deluded fantasies.

She glanced down. Three identical faces tipped up for a split second then dropped again. She shuddered. It was seriously weird looking at her own face and body on other people. But at least now she understood why the man inside thought she was his wife.

Well, kind of explained it. Evidently, his wife was the Goddess—goddess with a capital G, gauging by the emphasis they put on the word. And she figured it was a safe assumption that the Goddess was also her mirror image, just like the three girls paying homage to her pedicure. That left only a few niggling questions. First, where had the real Goddess gone? Second, how did she happen to have a tattoo identical to the Goddess's when it was a completely original design? And third, where the heck was she? Some bizarre country in Outer Mongolia?

She decided getting answers from her so-called husband would be her first choice. Going to the one he'd called the Wise One would be a backup, Plan B. "Okay, girls. Off your knees. You're going to get calluses . . . or scabs . . . or something."

The three servants all stood, shrinking from her attempts to touch them, and resumed a "how can we serve you" stance. She had a feeling if she told them to leap off the nearest bridge they'd do it without thinking. That made her feel very odd. Powerful, but also out of sorts.

"At ease, troops," she joked, trying to hide her discomfort. It was going to take some getting used to, speaking to her own face times three. "Don't sweat it. I . . . um, changed my mind." She forced a smile that she didn't exactly feel like producing. "I'll call you if I need anything." She backed into the room. Before she got far enough inside to shut the door, her backside bumped into something hard and warm, with a very curious protuberance at about her lower-back level.

"You're acting very strangely." Behind her, the man set his hands on her shoulders. His fingers worked the muscles of her neck, which suddenly felt like hard, painful lumps.

"Like I said, there is a reason for that." Knowing if she let him continue the shoulder rub, she'd be on the floor playing Hide-the-Protuberance in about three minutes flat, she took a large step forward then turned to face him. Her mouth worked, but nothing came out. Her gaze insisted on dropping to his very impressive cock. She blinked real slow, so that she saw more of the back of her eyelids than the naked man. Still, the words sat in her throat, hung up somewhere between her belly and mouth.

Whew, it would help immensely if he were dressed. And had a hood over his head so she couldn't see his unbelievably handsome face . . .

"What is it?" he asked.

. . . And if he talked through a synthesizer so his voice sounded like Alvin and the Chipmunks. Rodents did not make her wet and dizzy.

"I told you," she said, her eyes closed. "I'm not your wife.

Not. Your. Wife. I've never met you." She was on a roll, finally able to speak. Yay! Feeling brave, she opened her eyes and allowed her gaze to settle on his forehead—it was attractive while not being quite so distracting. "I don't even know your name, which I have to admit, is a first for me, since we just"—her gaze decided a forehead was not fertile ground and slid lower, to his full, pouty lower lip"—had the most incredible sex."

He didn't speak for a while, just stood there, head tipped a little, gaze drilling hers. Naked. Naked and yummy and curious. Or maybe intrigued. She couldn't be sure. All she could be sure about was that he liked something he saw, heard, smelled or tasted. The protuberance was still at full staff. Did it ever go down? Had he OD'd on the little blue pill?

"Anyway, if you could," she continued, trying hard not to think too much about the wonder of his never-ending erection. "I want to go home and I was hoping you'd answer some questions for me."

"Perhaps. But you will not leave." He crossed his arms over his scrumptious chest and rested a bulky shoulder against the wall.

Wasn't he going to sit down? Put some clothes on? Do something besides stand there buck naked and field questions like a Major League batter? She'd pitch. He'd swing . . . and score a home run.

She motioned toward a chair and he nodded, walked himself over to said chair and sat. Yes. That was a little better. At least now certain . . . things . . . weren't quite as distracting.

Since when was she so enamored by the sight of an erect penis?

She cleared her throat. "First, your name? Could you please tell me your name?"

"Xur, but you should know—"

"Okay. Good. Xur." At least now she could say she knew his name. First name only. But it was a start. Beggars couldn't be choosers. She'd get the nitty-gritty later . . . maybe . . . hopefully. "And what city are we in?"

"The city of Celestine."

"Celestine?" She rummaged around her brain, trying to recall where, if anywhere, she might have heard the name. Didn't strike her as familiar. Not at all. "I'm not the best at geography. Flunked every test in high school. Uh, could you tell me what state that's in? Arc we still in Michigan? Maybe in the Upper Peninsula?"

His eyebrows bunched together. "I haven't heard of this place, Michigan."

"Haven't heard of Michigan? Have you heard of North America?"

"North Ameri—? What?" he asked, looking like she'd just spoken to him in Swahili.

"The continent. North America," she said, enunciating.

"Huh?" He gave her a blank stare.

"Earth?" she tried desperately. Surely he knew Earth. They were on Earth! There wasn't such a thing as life on other planets. Or space travel.

"Earth?" he repeated, like it was the most foreign word he'd ever heard.

"Yes, Earth. Please. Tell me you have heard of Earth? Blue planet with cute white fluffy clouds. Third from the sun . . . or is it the fourth? I can never remember."

"Perhaps a visit to the Wise One would help," he suggested, standing.

Time for Plan B. She so didn't want to think about the possibility of missing work on Monday. What would Mr. Baudeur say? "Yes. Oh, yes. Let's go see the Wise One."

He beat her to the door, opened it and motioned for her to precede him. She paused. "Aren't you going to put on some clothes first?"

"Clothes?" He gave her another confused stare. Then he laughed. Oh, what shudders and shivers his rumbly chuckle birthed in her body. "How you delight me, wife. I'm so glad to have you back. Come, let's go speak with the Wise One. He'll help us both understand what's happened."

Eager to find out what planet she was on—she could think of very few places on Earth where men walked around stark nekkid in the streets in broad daylight, glory as it was—she hurried through the door and out into an expansive corridor that reminded her of a castle, or even the Catholic church her grandmother used to take her to when she was a kid. The beams on the ceiling reminded her of a whale's ribs, arching up to the center and meeting the spine that ran down the length. The walls looked like they were carved out of solid rock. Rough. Damp, she realized when she let her fingertips trail along as she walked. The air was damp, too, and smelled salty, like the sea.

After following Xur a mile or two—or so it felt—they entered a huge room filled with people. Immediately she noticed a couple things. First, every woman in the place had her face, which was, like, weirder than her strangest dream ever! And every male was completely nude and sporting a hard-on.

Was this heaven or hell? How would a girl know?

When she took her first step into the room, everyone, man, woman and child, dropped to their knees and lowered their heads in homage.

Oh my God, it was strange.

She wrapped the blanket tighter around herself, not that she had anything to hide. Now that she thought about it, every woman in the place had her lumpy butt with a touch of stubborn cellulite. And every man in the place had seen it.

Gag! She tugged the blanket tighter.

"This way," Xur said. He took her hand. The touch gave her just the slightest sense of comfort. This was a strange, strange place. Shocking in so many ways, she was afraid to turn the next corner. At least with him at her side she didn't feel quite so alone.

She tipped her head to deliver a smile of appreciation his way. He deserved it.

He shot one back at her, although his wasn't exactly an innocent "you're welcome" type of expression. More like "you're welcome, now let's go back and get busy."

"Only a little further." He pushed open a huge door at the far end of the room and they stepped into yet another corridor. This one was, thankfully, much shorter. It led to a small, intimate room filled from floor to ceiling with books.

A young man sat at a desk, his head lowered over the thin, dusty pages of some enormous book.

"Wise One," Xur said, following Kylie into the room and closing the door behind him.

The young guy—who kind of resembled Kylie's mental picture of a surfer dude, long, shaggy blond hair streaked by the sun, tan skin—lifted his head and gave her a smile. She half expected him to greet Xur with a Southern Californian "Dude."

"The Goddess. It's good to see you. But I told you"—the yet-to-be-proven Wise One gave Xur a glare—"it's too soon. It isn't safe for her to return. What have you done?" The wise guy rounded the huge desk. Kylie was relieved to see he was wearing a little white wrappy thing around his hips, hiding his privates. As it was, she wasn't buying the whole Wise One thing. With his danglies hanging out in the breeze, she'd have an even harder time taking him seriously. Funny, she had no problems taking Xur seriously, dangly parts notwithstanding. "Leave us," he demanded, directing his command at Xur.

Xur didn't take the order too well. Clearly a man who was used to making demands, not abiding by them, he visibly gritted his teeth and glared at the Wise One. There was this little testosterone vibe, a silent pissing match. Xur didn't exactly lose, but he was the bigger man and accepted the fact that he had to leave. Kylie's respect for him swelled.

The second the door closed behind him, the Wise One/ surfer dude said, "Shit, I was hoping he wouldn't go dragging you back yet. I told those two assholes they could check up on you but couldn't touch you. Fucking dicks."

"Mind telling me what's going on? That man out there says I'm his wife but I sure as heck don't remember being married. And what's with the Goddess stuff? And while we're at it, why are there a bunch of women out there who look exactly like me? I mean, this whole thing is just plain scary!"

"Here's the score," the Wise One said, plopping his

white-wrapped butt on the desk. "Yes, you're married to Xur. You're the Goddess, you just don't remember, and we're both from the same place, you and me—Plymouth, Michigan. We went to school together, good old Pioneer Middle School. I'm sure you don't remember me . . ."

Where was this conversation going? She was married? Huh?

"Anyway, I always had this thing for you—thought you were hot. And I was working on this secret project for the government that I can't talk about when I discovered a portal to this . . . dimension or whatever you want to call it. Don't ask me to explain it again, because I've tried. You didn't get it. Anyway, the people here had some problems with . . . pro-creating, to put it politely. And well, the men needed women, vessels so to speak."

"Vessels for what?"

He gave her a guilty smile. "I had you cloned. Don't ask me how I got your DNA, 'cause I've tried to explain that, too. And I can't explain how your clones are all the same age as you are. Suffice it to say certain functions of life move at different speeds if I manipulate the portal, so your clones could leave Plymouth, Michigan, as infants yet enter Celestine as adults—"

Her head was spinning. Portals? Clones? Time warps? "Um—"

"Okay. Won't go there again, either. Yeah. Anyway, thanks to me, there are like hundreds of Kylie Mannings here. And you're the Goddess because, well, because I said so."

"So, if I'm the Goddess of this place, why don't I remember anything?"

"Because there's this group of people who aren't exactly happy with the arrangements here. Motherfuckers want you dead." He cleared his throat. "So, I sent you back to Plymouth, hoping you'd be safe there for the time being. Oh, and I had your memories erased. You know, for your protection."

"How very thoughtful."

"Hey, I tried." He didn't look the least bit apologetic, even though from the sound of it, he'd manipulated her life big-time, ferrying her back and forth between "dimensions," stealing her DNA, creating hundreds of copies of her . . . "Until you were sent back, you were quite happy with things here."

"Yes, well, I'm not sure what I feel right now," she said truthfully. None of it made any sense. Dimensions. Clones. People after her. Memories erased. There wasn't a bit of believability in any of it! Had she fallen asleep with the Sci Fi Channel on again? After a fierce pinch to her thigh failed to wake her up, she figured she had no choice but to go with the flow for now. If this was indeed a dream, she couldn't really be hurt or killed. Right? "Assuming you're telling me the truth, how long was I gone?"

"Oh, I'm telling you the truth all right. Time here moves at a different rate than back in Plymouth. Days on this side, years on yours." He cleared his throat. "So, now that we've had our little chat, I hope you're feeling better."

"Not really."

"Sorry. If it makes things any easier, the memories will come back. Over time."

"Time? I don't have time. I want to go home. My new job starts—"

"Not possible. At least not right now. I don't have the ability to open the portal yet—transporting three people at once drained the power supply—so you're going to have to hang low for a few, at least until it recharges."

"But my job—"

"Nothing I can do about it. Sorry. Now listen carefully. Until I can get these assholes taken care of, you'll just have to sit tight, stay out of sight. Don't worry. The leader's as good as dead. I know who he is. Just gotta find where he's hiding. Here's a thought, how about taking a second honeymoon? You can get reacquainted with that husband of yours." He winked.

Her head swam. Too much information. *Can't go home? Her job. A husband? A honeymoon? Someone wanted her dead? A husband?* Her cheeks heated. "He's really my husband? You're sure?"

"Positive. It's all legal and everything. I have proof," he said, hurrying back around the desk.

"No, no. That's okay. Call me crazy, but for some reason I believe you. But I have a question. Why do people want me dead?"

Now he looked guilty. He shifted nervously in his seat. His gaze dropped to the desktop. "It's sort of complicated."

"Try me."

"I guess you could call it professional jealousy. With my help, you sort of displaced someone else as reigning Goddess."

Finally, some hope of things returning to the "normal" she remembered. The life back in Michigan. The job she'd busted her ass to get. "No biggie. There we go! A solution.

Tell the former Goddess she can have her goddessness back. No hard feelings. And I'll go back to Plymouth and live the life I *remember*, just like I want to. It's a win-win situation, except for maybe you—"

He shook his head. "It's not that simple. You see, the only way a Goddess can be removed from her throne is by death."

She swallowed a boulder-sized lump in her throat. "You mean you killed her? For me? I didn't ask you to do that!"

"No, you didn't *ask*, *you* killed her."

"Huh?" That lump swelled to the size of a semi truck. "No way! I'm not a killer. I don't kill people. Heck, I don't kill insects." She fanned her flaming face. Just the thought of her killing someone was shocking. He couldn't make her believe she killed someone. No, no, no! A lie. It had to be a lie!

"It was an accident, when you came out of the portal."

An accident! Okay, that she could accept a little better. She'd killed the Goddess. Kind of like Dorothy killed the witch in *The Wizard of Oz*. "So, if it was an accident, why are these people so hell-bent on revenge?"

He shrugged. "Because that's the way of this place. A life for a life."

She was so not liking this place! Then something he said earlier played back through her mind. Life for a life? "These people kill anyone who kills, regardless of whether it's by accident or not. And you're going to kill their leader?"

"I have no choice. With him gone, the others should surrender."

She didn't need any crystal ball to see trouble was brewing. For both of them, Goddess and Wise One. "I don't like this. Send me back to Plymouth. Send me back now."

"I told you, I can't. Not until the solar cells recharge. In case you haven't noticed, this place isn't exactly the most technologically advanced culture in the universe. Can't even get a pack of AA batteries when you need them. You're stuck here for now. And you're in danger. So, before they find you, you need to hustle out of here. Word has spread already. Several people know you've returned."

"Shit, shit, shit! I don't like this at all. I have no control. None whatsoever. I have one last question."

"Shoot."

"I gotta know, what did you get out of all this? Why'd you do it in the first place?"

"Why?" He sat, kicked his feet on the desk and flashed a Cheshire cat smile. "I was merely a man in Detroit, Michigan. Here, I'm practically a god. The revered Wise One. With an abundance of very willing you-clones. Simply put, I'm in heaven."

Kylie shuddered. Too much information there, too.

"Now, go, hide. Do the Goddess thing. I'll send word when it's safe to return to the palace. In the meantime, I'll tell that husband of yours where I want you hidden—and I know he'll take matters into his own hands if you refuse to cooperate." The slimy smile he gave her made her want to puke, even though she had a notion that any discipline Xur decided to dole out would be more pleasure than punishment.

Chapter 3

Kylie had to give it to the Wise One, his idea of an appropriate hiding place for a Goddess was first-rate. Not quite the Fairmont, but the so-called cottage was not only huge but also incredibly beautiful, with a lush flower garden surrounding the entry. The sweet scents of lavender and roses filled her nostrils as she followed Xur into the mammoth building through a door tall enough and wide enough to fit an elephant. An armed guard stood beside the door, motionless, like a statue, a toy. He didn't even blink.

The second Kylie stepped inside, she grew breathless again. They stood inside a giant hallway with high ceilings and rich fabrics draped over the walls. Rich red. Deep purple. It made the place look like a medieval New Orleans bordello, but classier. Kylie had the urge to sing "Lady Marmalade." *Voulez-vous coucher avec moi ce soir*. Dressed in a bejeweled bikini like her maids had been wearing back at the palace, and following a man who was still completely nude, with an adorable butt—she'd noticed *that* quite some time ago—she felt saucy, a little reckless and wild. The journey to their hiding place—made on foot!—had taken quite a while, many hours. She'd played the role of servant to Xur, while strategically hiding her tattoo with a white cape that hung from her shoulders. The long walk had given her a chance to sort out the information the Wise Ass had dumped on her.

Wise One, her butt! Yes, she was steamed! He'd effed her life, dragging her through portals, making a bazillion clones without her permission, erasing her memory, risking her new job! And why? So he could fuck her a million times over! She couldn't wait to get the hell out of this place. Men!

It was a good thing she was outside reaching distance. Given the opportunity, there was no saying what she might do to him.

But she had to admit, despite being outraged, there was a part of her that was appreciating the finer aspects of being a goddess with a capital G for a day or two, particularly where it came to her chosen husband. Despite the fact that she had no recollection of marrying the man, there was something between them, a current of energy that sizzled in the air when they were near each other, as well as a sense of comfort and trust. It was a very strange thing for her, to trust a man she really didn't know. In the normal world, she didn't trust men at all, even the ones she knew very well.

They filled the hours walking, engaged in friendly chatter. Xur Phoenix—she finally knew his last name!—was trying hard to help her remember him, their life together in Celestine. And make her forget the one she had back in Plymouth. It almost made her feel guilty that she couldn't.

"A bath?" Xur asked, leading her through a series of smaller hallways into a gorgeous room also swathed in heavy fabrics and sporting what had to be the world's largest bed dead in the center of the floor. "Or food first?" He took both her hands in his and pulled her toward the bed, dusting each of her fingertips with a little kiss. "Mmmm. You must be starved. I'll ring for food." He reached for a cord at the head of the bed.

Kylie's stomach rumbled, casting its vote. "Sure. Okay. Maybe I could take a bath while we're waiting?" A knock sounded at the door. "Already? Wow! What service."

Minutes later she was nude, soaking in a steamy tub full of scented water and munching on sweet, juicy fruits and admiring her husband's finer assets. She even let herself forget about her job for a while. Surely, once her boss discovered she was missing, he wouldn't hold missing a day or two of work against her. Being kidnapped couldn't be cause for dismissal.

Maybe she wouldn't kill old Wise Butt after all. When the aches in her legs and feet had faded, the rumbling hunger in her belly sated and the bathwater tepid, she stepped out, accepting a towel from a Kylie clone. Her skin tingled as she toweled off. The whole time she'd been bathing, there'd been the sense of expectancy. Xur had sat patiently, not rushing her, but there was something in his eyes, a hunger she hadn't been able to ignore. It made him look fierce, like an animal. She practically expected him to pounce on her the moment she was out of the water. The anticipation made her shiver.

"Are you chilled?" He looked worried. That made her feel all soft and girly inside. He genuinely cared about her.

"Oh, no. Not at all." She stood, cold water still dribbling from her wet hair, about ten feet from him and the bed. That was a big bed all right. And a big man. Big, hard cock, too. She shivered again, not because she was scared or cold. There was nothing to be scared of. Nothing at all. And she sure wasn't cold. In fact, her pussy was tingly. Warm, moist and getting hotter by the second. So was the rest of her.

He closed the distance between them, took her hand and led her to the bed. "Come. I'll keep you warm." The suggestion in his voice told her the double entendre was intentional.

She didn't resist. What woman could? He lay on the bed and pulled her on top of him. But before she could get comfy, he did a logroll, landing her flat on her back with him on top. His face hovered over hers. His panting breaths warmed her cheeks. His fiery gaze warmed her other parts. She squirmed underneath him. There were some parts that burned to be touched and she was determined to put them in contact with him one way or another.

"Goddess help me, but I can't resist you. I know you have no memory of me, and I'm trying to be patient, but I can't help myself. I want to fuck you."

"To hell with patience. I want you to fuck me, too."

He grinned, licked his lips and she watched, recalling what that tongue had done to her body, her nipples, her pussy earlier. "You know, I haven't yet punished you for leaving."

"Hey, according to your Wise One that wasn't my fault."

He caught both her hands in his and pinned them over her head. "I know that now," he said, his lips brushing over hers as he spoke. "But I figured I wouldn't hold it against you, since you're so fond of being disciplined."

This time the shiver was more like a shudder. Head to toe, she quaked. A wash of heat cascaded down her body, churning between her legs.

"Uh—"

He pressed his mouth to hers, kissing her breath away. His tongue slipped between her parted lips, probing her mouth while he gathered her wrists in one hand and used the other to explore parts of her anatomy that were quite pleased to have a visitor. He rolled her nipple between his thumb and forefinger. It was glorious agony. Little blades of pleasure-pain razored out from her nipple, skittering along her spine. Her pussy clenched around its own emptiness. She rocked her pelvis back and forth against him, trying to grind away the ache growing between her legs.

He broke the kiss and trailed little nips and licks along one side of her neck. Dying to drag her fingertips down his bare chest, to feel the crisp hair sprinkled over satin-soft skin, she wriggled her hands, struggling to break free from his grip.

"Oh, no you don't." He tightened his grip on her wrists until she yelped, then loosened it only slightly. "You may be the Goddess, but in private, I'm the Master." He sat up, left her for a moment.

Dazed and feeling alone, she rolled onto her side and watched him as he walked to an armoire and opened the doors. She could see inside, lots of leather strappy-looking things. Floggers maybe? Leather bindings? He returned to her with armfuls of stuff. His face flushed, his cock at full staff—and looking quite scrumptious, she could add—he dropped the goodies on the bed and flashed her a grin that made her heart hop in her chest. She sat up to inspect what he'd brought over, but he gave her a stern shake of the head and pointed at the mattress.

"Lie down," he demanded.

Turned on by the sharp tone of his voice, she gladly flopped back onto the bed. This incredibly sexy, strong man was her husband. Husband! The mind boggled. She felt like she was sleeping with both a stranger and an old friend at the same time. On one hand, she didn't know what he'd do next, which made her jumpy and jittery. On the other, she was so comfortable with him, she wasn't afraid to explore, to have fun, to give in to the hunger building up inside her. She felt so free, so happy, so . . . alive!

"Over on your stomach," Xur demanded, his voice dripping with sexual promise.

Trembling, dizzy with the need for release, she complied.

He grabbed her ankles and pulled, dragging her across the bed until her hips were at the edge of the mattress and her feet were on the floor. Her barely covered ass was up there, front and center. And she was one very happy Goddess.

"I haven't spanked you in a long time," he said, grazing her shoulders with something soft and tickly. She fought back a shiver. "Would you like me to spank you?"

"Oh . . ."

"Is that a yes?" He dragged whatever it was he had up

around the back of her neck, then down her spine to her bottom.

This time she couldn't help shuddering. "Yes," she squeaked.

"Mmmm." He lifted the toy away. "Have you forgotten how to address me?"

"Uh . . . yes, please?" she offered, not sure what he meant.

He tsked her and pressed his hot, yummy bod against her back. His erect cock poked at the material barely covering her ass. He whispered in her ear, "I will remind you only once more. Master. I am your Master when we are in our bed."

"Yes. Of course. You did say that, didn't you. Sorry . . . er, Master." This "Master" thing was new and strange to her, but oh, so much fun! She'd never ever role-played in bed but she'd always wanted to try. Yay, this was going to be great! She could literally feel the pulse of blood rushing to her pussy. Her heart was pounding against her ribs like a jackhammer. She was giddy and dizzy and squirmy. So hot. So, so hot.

"Much better." His voice was low and rumbly, like a bear. She really liked the way it sounded. It made her feel safe and happy and sexy. "If anything hurts too much, or you want me to stop, say . . . Michigan."

"Michigan?"

"Yes, Michigan," Xur repeated. Standing behind her with Kylie draped over the edge of the mattress, her rear end facing him, he pulled her towel down, down, down. Off her bottom, down her trembling legs. He left it on the floor at her feet.

"Ohhhhh. Okay," she said breathlessly. Every part of her body tingled with pent-up sensual energy. The anticipation of being spanked was like a drug, so intense, so exquisite. Her heart was knocking against her rib cage like a fist. Her head was swimmy and foggy. Her nerves tight and jittery. She hadn't known it would be like this. Had never guessed.

She heard the light *whap* of leather striking skin before she felt the sting of the impact. Caught her by surprise. She jumped, gasped and fisted the coverlet. The skin of her buttocks stung good. It was the most magnificent pain. The second one landed in a different spot, warming the skin there. And the third struck lower. Her fanny was on fire — in a wonderful way. Her whole body was sizzling with erotic energy. Her knees were wobbly. She pulled on the coverlet, worried she'd sink to the floor.

Being the gentleman he clearly was, Xur didn't let her fall. He kissed her stinging skin then helped her up onto the bed and onto her back. His expression was tight, jaw rigid, as he looked down on her, his eyes full of raw wanting. He ran his hands down her torso, following the motion with his eyes. The way he looked at her, like she was the most beautiful, sexiest woman in the universe. Like he could hardly contain his need for her for another second. It made her body ache everywhere. In a very good way. Before she could beg for relief from the agony he was stirring in her body, he kneeled over her, settled his hips between her legs and thrust his cock deep inside.

The air escaped her lungs in a quick whoosh. At precisely the same time, her body launched like a rocket toward climax. His quick rhythmic thrusts were exactly what her body craved. Muscles coiled tight. Heat surging through her veins.

As if he knew instinctively what she needed, he shifted his weight, sitting up until her entire body was uncovered. He pushed her knees apart and back and drew rapid circles over her clit.

He stopped a bazillionth of a second before she reached orgasm. Pulled that yummy cock out of her pussy. Quit stroking her clit. "No!" Only one more thrust of his cock would've done it. Sent her to that happy place where sensations blurred together and nothing but pulsing bliss existed. Not even a full thrust would've been needed. A half stroke. A twitch might've even done it for her. She wanted to scream, the frustration was so intense. She tipped her hips, desperately hoping he'd get the hint. "Not more punishment. Please, no more."

"Oh no, my Goddess. I'm not punishing you now," he said, laughter lifting his voice. He sounded too cheerful for her. Way too damn cheerful. What was he so freaking happy about? "I'm rewarding you."

Rewards were good reasons to be happy, though she wasn't exactly feeling rewarded at the moment. "Reward?"

"Oh, yes. Reward." He motioned toward the forgotten collection of goodies he'd brought over from the armoire. "We can't let all this stuff just sit here unused, can we?"

"Oh. No. I suppose not." She glanced at the pile of sex toys. Outside of a plastic vibrator, she had no idea what those thingies were. Lots of chrome-plated doohickeys. And black leather. Mmmm. Her internal generator was revving up again, creating a whole lot of heat.

"On your knees," he commanded, as he scooped up a small white cardboard box. Looked a lot like the kind of jewelry box you might get with the purchase of some junk jewelry from a discount store.

Curious, a little wobbly, and really, really warm, Kylie forced herself upright, on her knees on the mattress. Between her near-boneless state and the mattress's shifting as Xur moved, it was no small feat holding her position.

"Very nice," he practically purred. He flipped the top off the box and pulled out a narrow silver chain. Or rather, what looked like three chains fastened together. A small alligator clamp hung from the end of each one. The little grippy parts were covered with what looked like black rubber.

What the heck was it?

He held two of the little clips in his hands and stared hungrily at a point about eight inches or so south of her chin. Didn't take her long to figure out where those to clamps were headed. But what about the third one?

Just because he had to figure it would nearly kill her, he bent his head and swirled his tongue around each nipple. They stood out, erect and sensitized. Then he clipped the ends of the chains first to one, then the other.

Oh, God! The sweet agony! It pinched just enough to feel really, really good.

"How're you liking your reward so far?" He smiled at her with such an evil fire in his eye, she thought she might melt.

"Good," she squeaked. She sucked in a gasp when he tugged gently on the chain. Oh, he was a mean, mean man! Mean in such a very nice way. Still had no idea where that third clamp went.

Still holding the one loose end of the chain, he rolled onto his back. "Straddle my face. I want to eat you."

The promise heavy in those words made her whimper. And the little yank he gave the chain made her do more than that. She shuddered, crawled on hands and knees until her pussy was positioned over his mouth. She heard him audibly inhale.

"You smell so good." His voice was husky. Ubermale. Sensuous. He reached up and gripped her hips. His fingertips dug into the soft flesh. He pulled down until she was literally sitting on his face. His nose rubbed up against her pubic bone. His lips, tongue and teeth performed magic on her clit.

Her legs were trembling. She bent over at the waist and supported her upper body with her outstretched arms. "Oh. My. God." She felt the bite of the little clamp on her clit. Her eyeballs bulged. She could feel them. She straightened up and the chains connecting her nipples and clit pulled against one another, tugging simultaneously on all three places. Minibolts of pleasure-pain arced through her body like zaps of electricity. She gasped. "Xur!" Afraid to move, afraid the amazing sensations would become too intense, she froze in position, her pussy hovering over his face. Her shoulders hunched down a bit to keep the chains from pulling too hard.

"Shoulders back," he demanded. "It'll feel so much better that way."

"Oh God, oh God, oh God!" She slowly pushed her shoulders back. The chains tightened again, pulling at her nipples and clit. Another series of hot, intense bursts of pleasure shot through her body.

Then he stared fucking her pussy with his tongue and

those short, staccato surges lengthened and smoothed out into long, languid waves.

While he fucked her pussy with his tongue, she slowly rocked her hips, intentionally increasing and decreasing the pull on the clamps. Such sweet agony! Like nothing she'd ever felt before. She wanted to come but at the same time wanted the tension coiling tight inside her to keep building, building, building until she couldn't stand it anymore. She knew the choice was not hers to make. Xur would decide. That realization made her even hotter. Even more desperate for release.

He lifted her hips, and holding her up, slid out from under her. She didn't object, knowing in her heart that whatever he had planned next would be even better. "Down on your hands and knees."

Yes, oh yes. She loved being fucked doggy-style. Quivered with delight when he scooted around her back end on his knees and took her hips in his hands again.

The mattress shifted as he reached to the side for something. A soft click and hum told her what it was before she felt the cool plastic tip probing the cleft between her ass cheeks. It was not quite in the right place . . .

"Lower," she whispered. She lifted her fanny, hoping to guide the vibrator closer to her pussy.

"No. That's not where I'm aiming."

A gulp of air lodged itself in her throat. Nothing as large as a vibrator had ever been in her ass. Anal beads, yes. The little teeny, tiny beads. A fingertip. That too. But not a dildo. Or a cock. And at the moment, she wasn't sure if she wanted to keep it that way or not.

She felt him spreading something cool and wet around her anus. It dribbled down toward her pussy and she reflexively clenched her inner muscles, curled her back and tucked her bottom down. The soft buzzing vibrations hummed around her hole. That felt good. Better than good. She wondered what it would feel like to have those yummy pulses inside her ass while he fucked her pussy.

Maybe she had been a little hasty about the vibrator?

"I know how much you love this."

"I do?" Had she . . . had he . . . ? She wished her memory would come back.

"Oh yes, especially this part. When I enter you oh, so slowly," he murmured in a low, silky voice that made her think of decadent chocolate. Smooth and rich and yummy. He pushed a little harder and the very tip of the vibrator slipped inside her anus. The buzzing flowed over her skin, penetrated inside to create the most amazing, sensual sensation.

So close. So close to orgasm her body was tight like overstretched rubber bands. Ready to snap. To explode.

He eased the vibrator deeper inside. So good. So fucking good she couldn't breathe. Her arms shook. Her chest fell to the bed. She didn't care that her face was buried in blankets.

Then he thrust his cock inside her pussy. It was so intense. Buzzing vibrations in her ass. Thick cock in her pussy. She arched her spine and tossed her head backward. The clamps pulled at her nipples, her clit, sending jagged, glorious pulses of pleasure up and down her spine. She heard herself screaming. Heard the *slap, slap, slap* of his thighs striking her fanny as he fell into a steady rhythm. But all that mattered was the vibration deep inside and the intimate strokes of his cock.

Her orgasm washed over her like a hot wave. *Whoosh*, up her body. She relished every moment, measured in loud, thudding heartbeats. And she rejoiced when Xur shouted his release and slowed his thrusts to deep, penetrating movements that drove his cock and seed up against her womb.

Slick with sweat, he dropped onto the mattress. His breathing was ragged and fast. She closed her eyes, turned onto her side, wrapped her arms around his neck and held him, loving the weight of him, the warmth when he log-rolled her onto her back. Pushing up on outstretched arms, he kissed her nose. Her forehead. Her chin. Then he gently removed the vibrator and the delicate chains and clamps and set them aside.

"My Goddess. My life. I have nothing if I don't have you." He combed his fingers through her hair.

She closed her eyes and smiled, inhaling deeply, drawing in the musky-sweet scent of man and sex. "And I . . . I . . . Oh my God." For the first time in her life, she knew. This was the man for her, the one who made her whole. An image flashed through her mind, a memory. Of them together, like this, holding each other after having made love. Of Xur stroking her hair and promising he would never leave her side. He'd love and protect her forever.

She remembered!

It wasn't a lifetime of memories, no. Just a single blip. A moment. Whatever. But she remembered something. Something important and special and wonderful. She remembered how loved she'd felt then. How cherished and contented and whole Xur had made her. That was all she ever needed to remember. If nothing else came back, she didn't care. Xur loved her. Xur cherished her. He was strong yet gentle. He had earned her trust and had possessed her heart. And she was the luckiest damned Goddess in the universe.

So happy, contented, she could weep, she let herself relax, just enjoy the simple pleasure of being held.

But her peace was interrupted by a loud crash, and then shouting. Xur jerked on top of her before rolling off and jumping to his feet.

A man she knew, a man she'd slept with, burst into the room, arm raised, a knife in his fist. He charged at the bed, bloodlust in his eyes.

"Adam?" she murmured.

"Sorry, but it's our way," Adam said. "I tried to convince you to marry me, back in that other world, that place called Michigan. But you refused. All I wanted was to be husband to the Goddess. But you couldn't be bothered. And you didn't have the decency to stay in Michigan so a new Goddess could be selected. Now you must die."

Chapter 4

There were a lot of things about the past twenty-four hours that had taken Kylie Mannings by surprise. A kidnapping. Learning she was a Goddess. Discovering she lived in an alternate dimension where all the women were her mirror image. Finding out she had a husband.

The shocking nature of all those discoveries paled in comparison to learning her ex-boyfriend wanted her dead. In her life she'd had some ugly breakups, but this one took the cake—the whole bakery, in fact!

While she sat naked on the bed, gaping in silent horror, her husband did the hero thing and charged into action. He literally threw himself at Adam. Adam was ready for him, though, and was able to dodge him much too easily for Kylie's comfort. That knife raised in the air, cold determination on his face, he ran at Kylie like a butcher after a runaway hen. As any sane woman would do, she ran. Of course, she couldn't go far, since the one and only exit was behind him.

Luckily, before Adam caught her, Xur tackled Adam from behind and knocked him to the ground. There was much scuffling and grunting. Male arms and legs swinging. Kylie inched her way around the wrestling men, hoping to make it to the door where she could call for help. As was her luck, she didn't make it. A hand closed around her ankle, snapped around it like a sprung trap. It took her by surprise, as she was moving pretty fast, and made her lose her balance. Before she knew it, she too was in the midst of the melee, pushing, shoving, struggling to break free. She held her own—a feat, considering she'd never thrown a punch in her life. At one point she even managed to break free altogether. She scrambled on all fours from Adam. But seconds later he had her again.

Not once, not twice, but three times something belted her hard, on the back. The pain was unbelievable. It felt like she'd been clobbered with a huge metal club. Within minutes she felt herself getting tired. Bone weary. Heard Xur's voice, but she was too exhausted to struggle anymore. She wanted to go to him but she needed to rest. Her eyelids fell shut and the world faded away. It was so unfair! She'd finally found him again, and now he was lost.

Her husband. Her Master.

Xur brutally yanked the blade out of the man's chest and threw it across the room. He dropped to his knees at Kylie's side.

Was she . . . ?

"Oh, Goddess!" he murmured.

She was so still. Dark blood oozed from the three wounds on her back. The ugly marks marred her smooth, perfect skin and stirred rage anew. His hands shook, his whole body trembled with a bitter mixture of anger and dread.

He glared for a split second at the bastard who lay about ten feet away, eyes wide open in a death stare. He got what he deserved. How dare he attack the beloved Goddess!

His anger cooling, his fears and sorrow swelling in its place, Xur covered his own face, dropped his head and pressed an ear to her back. Would he hear the soft whoosh of air entering her lungs? Or would he hear dead silence?

He held his breath and waited, every muscle in his body trembling.

Nothing. He heard nothing!

"No," he heard himself say. Hot tears streamed from his eyes. This was his fault! If only he'd left her where she was, in that strange world she'd called Michigan. She would've been safe there. His fault. Why, oh why, hadn't he listened? The Wise One had warned him. Now the woman he loved more than life itself was . . . was . . .

He heard something! The softest, most wonderful sound. Air passing to her lungs.

"Praise the Goddess!" She was breathing, but barely. He carefully rolled her over and looked at her face.

Her face was so pale, her lips white. He shouted his relief and jumped to his feet. Help. He needed help. Now. He couldn't let his Goddess die, his life. His love. He shouted as he ran out into the hall. A healer. He needed a healer.

Immediately. He would never again doubt the words of the Wise One. And he would never again take the dangers of being the Goddess for granted. If she lived, he would protect her with his very life . . . he would send her back to Michigan, if that was what it took.

He would live without her, if it meant she would be safe and happy. That was all he wished for. He wished for her to be safe and happy.

Since she'd returned, he'd been trying to ignore the obvious—she didn't belong to his world anymore. She didn't belong to him. No man could possess a Goddess.

The alarm wrenched Kylie from her dreamless sleep. Her head buried under pillows, she thrust a hand out and blindly smacked at the air, aiming for the snooze button. On the fifth try, she hit it. The obnoxious buzz ceased and she tried to slip back to sleep for another nine glorious minutes.

Unfortunately, even though her body wanted at least another hour of sleep, her mind wouldn't let her have another minute. She stared at the clock. It was 7:02. More importantly, she was at home. In her house. Lying in her bed. Staring at her alarm clock.

Had that whole clone/alternate-dimension thing been a dream? Had to be.

"Oh, man!" She flung her arm at the nightstand and picked up her cell phone. What day was it? Was it Sunday? Monday? Her back ached. Her muscles were stiff, sore. Had she been sick? Or hurt? The dream had been so vivid, just like the dreams she tended to have when she was ill.

Sunday. It was Sunday. What a relief! At least she wouldn't have to rush to get ready for work. She could just stay in bed, rest. Yes, oh yes. That sounded wonderful. Her back was so sore. What had happened? Did those teenage trick-or-treaters attack her?

She sat up and tried to stretch. Man, what'd they do to her? Beat her up and leave her for dead? How'd she get into bed? She noticed she was nude and shuddered. Had they . . . raped her? She pulled the sheet around herself and glanced at the window. The drapes were partially parted in the center, letting a couple of inches of bright sunlight into the room.

It was so quiet. She felt so alone, and for once being alone didn't feel all that great. Maybe her imaginary husband, Xur, had been a dream, but—God help her—she missed him. Was that possible? To miss someone who didn't exist?

And another thing, she missed who she was when she had been with him, too. In her dream, he'd pulled something out of her somehow, a smidge of recklessness, a hunger for life.

Alone. She was alone. Awake. Xur was gone. Didn't exist. Ugh.

She rolled onto her belly and covered her head with a pillow. Maybe if she fell back asleep, she'd resume the dream. She'd done that once or twice in her life. It might happen. She closed her eyes and concentrated on visualizing Xur's adorable face. His dark eyes and hair. The cute cleft in his chin. "Come on, dream. Come back to me."

Despite the fact that most sound and light were snuffed out by feathers wrapped in 800-thread-count cotton, and she was concentrating on reviving a dream that was fading fast from her memory, she heard the knock on her front door. The hairs on her nape tickled. Who could be here this early on a Sunday morning? Was she imagining things? She jerked, throwing the pillow off, and listened. Yes, there was a knock. A loud, urgent pounding.

She jumped into a pair of sweats and a sweatshirt then hurried down to answer the door.

She peered through the peephole. It couldn't be! Could it? Was that man, dressed head-to-toe in police regalia, Xur? Impossible!

She unlocked the door and swung it open. "Wha—!" Her heart jumped around in her chest like an overwound toy. Her eyes burned. "It's . . . you're real?" she whispered, afraid she'd dozed off and her own voice might wake her up any minute. And then she'd discover he was gone again, a figment of her overactive imagination.

"I found you! Thank the Goddess. I was afraid I wouldn't be able to." He was grinning literally ear-to-ear. "Can I come in?"

"Tell me I'm not dreaming." She staggered backward until her backside hit the sofa table.

"You're not dreaming." He shut the door then closed the distance between them in one long stride. A cloud of coconut-scented air followed him.

Pinching herself, Kylie sniffed the air. She threw her arms around his neck and pressed her cheek to his chest. Real. He was real! He was there. With her. "How? What's going on? And why do you smell like coconuts? I thought you were gone forever. I thought I'd never see you again."

"I found the Suave scented liquid. I like it." His eyes

glittered. His hands were restless on her back, wandering up and down.

"I see that." She giggled, couldn't help it. She pulled out of his embrace for a second, just to get a good look at him again. The man was macho beyond compare but smelled like he'd bathed in coconut-scented suntan lotion. Adorable. He was so adorable. And sexy. And real! Her heart felt like it had swelled to ten times its normal size. "But how'd you . . . was that whole Celestine thing a dream? I'm so confused."

He gently led her to the couch, sat next to her and glued his big brown eyes to hers. Yes, those were real eyes. And those were real shoulders there under that blue short-sleeved uniform, and a real chest. Very real. Just because she could, she ran an index finger down his arm, traced the line of his biceps down to his elbow.

Her tummy did a flip-flop.

"How did this happen?" she asked again. "You're here. With me. Here. Real. I can't believe this."

"Yes, I'm here. With you. We're together."

"How?"

His gaze dropped to their joined hands. "I went to the Wise One and asked him to send you back to Michigan. Without me."

"You . . . you did? You wanted me sent away?" She pulled her hands from his. "Why? You didn't even ask me what I wanted," she whispered. She didn't understand. Why would he do that? Hadn't he said he loved her? Why was everyone making decisions for her? Without giving her a chance to say what she wanted! This was getting old. Real fast.

"I wanted you to be safe. Watching that bastard . . .

stab . . ." He visibly swallowed. "I couldn't live with the knowledge that it could happen again," he continued in a shaky voice. "It was my fault he'd found you. I brought you back when I shouldn't have. But I missed you . . . so . . . much . . . I couldn't stand being away from you any longer."

She could see he was struggling to talk. He gave her a watery smile that didn't get anywhere near his eyes. His hands fisted and flexed but he didn't lift them, didn't try to touch her again.

"I'm sorry, Goddess. I'm sorry for being so damn selfish, for not thinking of your safety first. I tried to fix it. I mean, I couldn't take away what had happened, but I could prevent it from happening again. Thankfully your injuries were superficial. After seeing you were tended to by the healer, I went to the Wise One, told him I wanted you to be safe, happy. If that meant I had to live without you, then that was the way it would be. I would deal with it. Somehow."

She could sense how difficult that would've been for him. The depth of his love, the scope of his sacrifice, it was difficult to comprehend. But it was there for her to see now, reflected in his eyes. It made his decision a whole lot easier to accept. It made something else a whole lot easier to accept as well—the urge to let it all go for the first time in her life. To let someone else take care of her, to make decisions, to be her Master. There was no way he'd ever make a decision that would hurt her. She had no doubt. This was a man she could trust. In all ways. She could trust enough to be herself, to do the one thing she'd always wanted to do but feared— she could relinquish control. In the bedroom and in her life.

"You did that? For me?" she whispered. "Even though you were sad when I was gone?"

"I had to."

She'd never known anyone who was capable of such self-sacrificing love. Not even her own mother. The closest she'd ever seen was her grandmother, who'd died years ago. It was wonderful. The most profound joy swelled inside her. "I don't know what to say."

"When I went to the Wise One, I told him my decision. He took you away, told me to leave him, return in one hour. I did as he told me to. Next thing I knew, he was telling me he'd found me a job as a police officer. Then he shoved me through a strange-looking door and I found myself here, in this odd but wonderful world. It took me hours to find you, but I did."

"So you're really here to stay?"

He ran his palm down her arm then hooked a finger under her chin. "You forgive me? You're happy? Happy I'm here with you?"

"Happy? Happy! I'm ecstatic!" She threw her arms around his neck and squeezed. He hugged her back with equal enthusiasm. She tipped her head to look into his eyes. "And yes, I forgive you."

His smile was so warm and genuine, it made her insides all whooshy and soft. She nuzzled his neck. His scent, combined with the way his body felt pressed against hers, made her insides all tingly and warm. Her nipples tightened into hard little nubs. Little zaps of heat charged through her body.

"Good." He kissed her forehead, grazed her bottom lip

with his thumb. She resisted the urge to nibble it. "We will start over, from the beginning, since you don't have any memories of our courtship. I have to admit, I'm a man who enjoys the chase—"

"The beginning?" she repeated, losing the battle. She let her tongue slip out and tease the tip of his thumb with shy little swipes. "Not that I mind being the chase-ee, because that's fun, too, but the very beginning? Like, before-sex beginning?"

"Yes, the very beginning," he said around a chuckle that made her knees knock. He removed his thumb from her mouth and combed his fingers through her hair. The gentle tugging felt so good. "Before sex, before we met, before everything."

"Not that I want to butt heads with you already, but what if I don't like that idea as much as you do?" She was so not thrilled with his suggestion. For a couple reasons, but the most pressing at the moment was the slick warmth gathering between her legs. It wasn't six years, but they already shared a history of sorts, and she wasn't sure that tossing that away and starting from scratch was such a great idea. She liked what they had already. Besides, at the moment, she just wanted to be close to him, in all ways. She wanted him to hold her, to touch her, to possess her.

"Mmmm. What do you want?" he asked, gently pushing her back.

"What I want"—she pulled her upper arms out of his grip and gave him a coy grin—"is to start somewhere in the middle. Say, before 'I do' but after the *we do* . . . as in, we make love." She illustrated by tracing the line down the center of his buttoned shirt, over his belt, to the bulge front and center behind the zipper of his pants. "I . . . missed you, too. And I don't want to go back to being strangers. I want this. I want us. I want to go forward."

"I see." He sounded a little breathless. "Very well. I will allow you this small concession." He stood.

"Thank you," she said, working at his belt. "Would it be too much to ask . . ." When she had his pants unsnapped and unzipped, she was pleased to see his cock seemed to be happy to go along with her plan. "Do you think you could still call me goddess? I kinda liked it." She pushed down his pants and underwear. Black, snug, sexy.

"Sure, my goddess," he said in his deep, rumbly bear voice. He caught her wrist just before she wrapped her fingers around his erection. "On one condition." He slanted her a wicked grin that made her heart skip a few beats. "You call me Master. Now run!" Still sporting that grin, he pushed her from him. She squealed and sprinted across the living room, giggling like a goof. She got about five feet before he scooped her up into his arms and carried her into her bedroom.

"Oh!" She sucked in a surprised gasp when he laid her flat on her back on the bed and pushed a knee between her thighs.

Her girl parts sent out the welcome wagon. Her brain shut down.

Master. He wanted her to accept him as her Master. There was no man on Earth she could accept as Master but Xur. She tried to answer, tried to tell him that, but her tongue lodged itself somewhere in her throat. Nothing was getting past it. Air, sound, nada.

She guessed he interpreted her silence as acceptance, because before she knew it, they were both undressed and he was kissing her. His tongue was doing things no tongue should be able to do. Dancing in her mouth and stirring up potent lust. And in combination with lips, teeth, she could barely keep from throwing herself at him and begging for mercy.

"Do you accept me as your Master?" he repeated.

"Yes." She struggled to focus her eyes. She was light-headed and giddy, melting, trembling. A fever was building inside her and she wanted relief. Now. Not a half hour from now. Not even five minutes from now. She rocked her hips back and forth, grinding her wet pussy against his very erect cock. "To hell with the chase. I surrender. Take me," she begged between little teasing kisses and nips. When he didn't answer, she bit his shoulder.

He growled and pinched her nipple. "You have no idea how to surrender. But I will teach you."

She shuddered. Oh, the joy this man gave her! "Take me," she repeated.

"How soon you forget." He lifted his upper body off her, removed his mouth from where it had been just seconds before—her neck, where it was doing some wonderful things—and gave her a frown. "Master. I am your Master. And you must address me as such whenever we are in this room."

"Oh, yes. Master. How could I forget?"

He frowned. "To make sure you won't forget again, I am going to punish you." He lowered himself until his face was inches from hers. "This time, I'm going to bring you to the point of climax but I won't let you come," he whispered. "You may not come until I say so. You will never forget how to address me after tonight."

The sharp tone of his voice, packaged with the fire burning in his eyes and the promise in his words just about vaporized her.

"And to make sure you don't . . . take matters into your own hands at any point," he said, sitting up again. "I'm going to have to tie your wrists, like so." He caught both of her wrists and pinned them to the bed above her head. "Where are your restraints?"

"Uh. I don't have any."

"You must." It took him maybe three long strides to get to her closet. He grumbled something to himself as he sifted through her clothes. Finally, he returned with his handcuffs in one fist and the silk scarf she'd bought on a whim but never worn in the other. "These will do. For now. We will get you some more effective restraints later." He eyed the headboard, grunted in male satisfaction and then scooped her up and deposited her higher up on the mattress.

She gleefully watched his scrumptious muscles work as he secured her arms. Then she squirmed as he set about torturing her.

He started at her neck. Biting and nibbling until goose bumps covered every square inch of skin she possessed. Next, he focused his attention on her breasts. He kneaded them, pinched and pulled at her nipples, then laved at them like a cat drinking milk until her blood was like lava. It simmered in her veins, carrying heat to every part of her body.

He then kissed a path down her stomach but stopped just

before reaching her pussy. "Before I go any further, perhaps we should come up with a new safe word?"

"New? What?"

"Since we are now in Michigan, I don't suppose that one's such a good idea. You have an idea for another one?"

She dragged her heavy eyelids up and gave him a surprised stare. "Are you kidding me? You expect me to think? Now? I'm at death's door. I can't think now. You come up with one."

"Very well." He visibly searched the room. His face lit up as his gaze rested on her clock. "Sony."

"Great. Sony. Got it. Can I use it now?"

"Only if you wish me to stop."

"Yes. No. No, I don't. Commence the torture, Master. Please."

Being both cruel and kind, he complied. He pushed her legs apart and gave her pussy a long swipe with his tongue. Then he parted her labia and danced his tongue over her clit.

"Oh, God," she moaned. "Oh, God, ohgod, ohgod." She tossed her head from side to side. Climax was inevitable. The final telltale flash of heat swooped up her chest and over her face. She sucked in a breath and prepared herself for the glory that would be her orgasm.

And then he stopped.

Her pussy twitched but didn't spasm. Robbed!

"Argh!" she shouted. She lifted her head and gave her very bad husband a death stare. "Sony, Sony, Sony! That was not nice! Not. Nice. You better finish what you started, buster."

He gave her a death stare right back. "Talk to me like that, and I'll have to punish you more severely."

"Nothing could be worse than this," she whispered, making sure to say it quiet enough for him not to hear. Softened her expression, too. When he didn't say anything else, like, "Okay, you've suffered enough," she added, louder this time, "Seriously. I'm dying here. I was so close."

"Yet, you've forgotten the lesson I have tried to teach you."

"No . . ." She struggled to remember what that lesson was. It took her a few, but she finally regained the use of enough gray matter to remember. "No, I haven't forgotten. Master. I'm sorry. This is all very new. But I will try harder. I want to surrender to you. Surrender it all, my very life. You are my Master, in all ways."

He nodded his head, his expression softening. "I love you, my goddess. As your Master, I will take care of you for the rest of your days. Your needs will be mine. Your wishes. Your worries."

She blinked back a tear. She hated crying. "Thank you, for leaving your life on Celestine, for following me here." She smiled as she watched him climb onto the bed and kneel next to her legs. He looked at her with such warmth and love in his eyes. As she gazed into them, she saw the depth of his devotion. Of his commitment to her.

He genuinely loved her. Like, loved with all his heart and soul and spirit. With the kind of self-sacrificing dedication she'd never seen before from a man. She realized something else, too. She had been searching for him, long before she'd been taken back to Celestine. Longing for him. Missing him.

She needed him. He was her life. He made her the woman she was meant to be.

They shared a smile.

"I am yours," she whispered. "My life, my future, my everything. It's been such a short time but I feel like I've known you forever. I . . . love you. Thank you for coming. Thank you for finding me."

"And I love you, too, my goddess." He teased her slit with the head of his cock and she arched her back, anxious for him to enter her. "You are my life," he said. "Don't you see that yet? I didn't leave my life when I left Celestine. I followed it."

"Yes. I see that now. But you still left behind the world and life you knew to come here."

He hooked his fingers under her chin and stared into her eyes. "I followed you. To this wonderful place. We will be together for the rest of our lives. We will make a life together." He unfolded his hands, revealing the delicate chain she'd worn in Celestine. "I brought something for you."

"You did. I was afraid it had been lost. If you'll untie me—"

He shook his head. "I'll do the honors."

As she trembled and quaked with pent-up desire, he suckled her right nipple until it was a hard pink point. Then he clipped the first clamp to her nipple and moved on to the left.

It was as if there was a direct connection between her pussy and nipples. The pinch of the clamp sent little bursts of heat through her body, down between her legs.

"Spread your legs," he demanded. He held the third clamp between his finger and thumb.

She knew the intense pleasure-pain that last one would bring her. Whimpering, she parted her knees and sucked in her stomach.

He bent over, and releasing the chain, gently parted her labia to expose her clit. "Do you have a vibrator? I want to tease you a bit more first."

"More teasing?" she asked weakly.

"Yes, more. You deserve it for the lack of respect you show me. Vibrator."

Since her hands were secured up over her head, there wasn't any chance she could point to anything. Jerking her head to one side was the only option she had. "Nightstand drawer," she said.

Luckily for her, he got the drift. The mattress bounced when he hopped down to the floor, reminding her of the fact that she really, really needed a new mattress set. Impatiently, he rummaged through the drawer filled with magazines and whatever else she'd stuffed in there, until he found the little pink vibrator, no doubt at the very bottom of the drawer, in the back. "Aha!" he proclaimed, holding it up like it was some friggin' major discovery or something.

The man was really too cute. And too sexy. Mrrrowwww!

Giving her this hot, "I'm going to make you suffer" look, he returned to his position on the bed, twisted the bottom of the toy and adjusted the intensity of the vibrations to maximum speed. She could tell by the pitch of the hum. Her mouth went dry as she watched him smooth some lube on the tip. He wiped the excess on his cock. A couple strokes down to the base and then up to the tip. Oy, if he expected her to last more than two seconds before coming, he was in for a surprise.

"Goddess or not, you're still expected to respect me as your Master. Since your return, you've been sarcastic and willful, you've forgotten how to address me. I realize you've suffered the loss of your memory, but I intend to teach you quickly what it means to submit." He ran the very tip of the buzzing toy around her vagina, down toward her anus then back up toward her clit. Of course, because he wanted her to suffer, no doubt, he made sure to steer clear of her clitoris.

Her inner muscles clenched and unclenched as anticipation swept through her body. The pinching of her nipples worked to intensify the frustration.

Her husband was so mean! But she sure was enjoying it.

"So tell me now, goddess. Have you learned your lesson yet?" he murmured in that low, husky voice of his. He made another circle around her pussy with the vibrator, this time letting the tip skim across her clit. White-hot sparks of need scattered through her body. "Or do I need to punish you some more?"

"Ye-yes, Master." Her eyelids were too heavy to hold up. She let them fall closed. Her stomach tightened. She tipped her hips up, spread her legs wider.

"More punishment? Very well."

"No! No, Master. I meant no, you don't need to punish me anymore."

"I believe I do. I believe you want me to." This time he let the vibrator remain on her clit for several seconds, long enough to make her shake. Then he pushed the toy inside her pussy and applied the clamp to her clit.

She pressed her feet to the mattress and bucked, pushing her pelvis high into the air. The little sparks were now giant infernos and they didn't scatter like hot metal shards, they swept through her like explosions. "Eey! Ohhhh!" she screeched. The chains caught with her motion and tugged on both nipples and clit, creating even more intensity.

She was going to die! Her heart was going to race out of control, her lungs were going to collapse, and she was going to expire. Right there. "Oh, please, Master. Please!"

"Please what, goddess? Please more? Very well."

"No . . ." She opened her eyes.

He settled himself between her legs, squirted some lube onto her anus and then pushed a finger slowly into her hole.

Her anus burned a tiny bit as it stretched, but the pain was just one more sensation added to the already overwhelming flurry that she was swimming in. The sharp pinching at her nipples, clit. The sound of his groans as he stroked his cock. The vibrations deep inside her vagina. The sight of his tight expression as he looked down at her pussy.

He pulled his finger out. "Goddess, I can't wait another minute. I must fuck you. Now. In your ass."

She put up a silent prayer of thanks.

He entered her with a slow, deliriously decadent thrust. His cock filled her completely, stirring up the embers of the fire that he had allowed to die down. The rising heat spread out, out from her center, up her stomach, over her chest.

With each slow inward thrust, he drove her body closer, closer to release. And when she trembled on the verge of climax, he murmured in her ear, "That's it, love. Turn yourself over to me. Let yourself go. Come for me."

She sighed, overcome by the pleasure of her climax, and clung to him, wrapping her legs around his waist to welcome his cock deeper inside. Her pussy spasmed around the vibrator, and she felt his cock swell slightly as he found his release. It was glorious. It was beyond words.

When all the toys and paraphernalia had been removed, and she was lying a sated, tingling blob of delighted goo, she kissed his face, just as he had done after the first time they'd made love. His eyes. His nose. His chin and forehead. "My refuge. My protector. My friend. My Master."

"My naughty goddess." He stretched and groaned, like a large, sated man was prone to do. "Tonight, you will not surrender so easily. I want a real chase."

She squirmed, heating again at the thought of him chasing her around the house—correction, it was the thought of him catching her *after* chasing her through the house that had her squirming. "Fair enough."

"Good." He gave her a satisfied nod. "Then there's only one other matter to discuss."

"Oh?"

"That of our second wedding. I wish to set the date, so that we are able to make preparations. Since your memory of our first ceremony has been erased, I want this one to be special, a day you could never forget. What is the tradition here? In this world? In Celestine it is the groom's responsibility to plan the wedding. It is a very private event, attended by only the couple's very closest friends and family."

"The tradition here is the exact opposite. We get married in a church in front of hundreds of people. And the bride takes a good year or two to plan the wheres, whos and whens of it all, with the help of her maid of honor and mother. But this is what I'm thinking," she said, snuggling closer to his warmth. "I don't want a traditional wedding as much as I always thought I did. How about we forget about planning, and I'll take a week or two off work, and you surprise me? I have all the faith in the world that I'll love what you plan, just like I did before."

"As you wish, my goddess. As you wish."

"And then, afterward, I think I might need a little more of your very special brand of punishment. You know, because I'll probably need a reminder about respecting my Master. I hate to say it, but I think it could take a few weeks, months even, before I get it right." A grin pulling at her mouth, she jumped up from the bed and dashed for the door. "But you'll have to catch me first!"

His laughter rumbled down the hall after her. "How I love a good chase. Run, my naughty goddess. You will be punished," he said almost directly behind her, "when I catch you."